ENTICING THE ELF

ELF MAGIC
BOOK 2

LOUISA MASTERS

Enticing the Elf

Copyright © 2025 by Louisa Masters

Cover Photo: Wander Aguiar

Model: Ryan

Cover Design: Booksmith Design

Editor: Hot Tree Editing

ENTICING THE ELF

There's nothing I want more than a life with him… but my past is the world's worst wingman.

For a big chunk of my life, I expected to die along with the rest of my species. Nobody thought we'd make it, and I did my best to live in the now and enjoy every second of precious life.

Now that's coming back to bite me in the ass.

Because the impossible happened, and we got our second chance. A safe home. A tomorrow worth planning for. And a future I want to spend with Dáithí.

He's amazing—sassy, clever, the kind of guy who can cut you down with one eyebrow and still make you laugh. We've known each other a long time, and convincing him to date me was one of the best wins of my long life. Convincing him to be my boyfriend? That's a fight I might not win.

Because the reputation I earned when I was living life to the fullest has stuck, and Dáithí's convinced I'm only in this for a good time, not a long time. He's protecting his heart from future damage by keeping things casual between us… even though they're not.

How do I prove I want him forever?

CHAPTER ONE

Dáithí

THE ELEVATOR DOORS OPEN, the same way they do a million times every day, and I give myself a second to finish sending the email memo telling staff that the hallways are not to be used for putt-putt golf. Not that I think office golf is a bad idea—I took part in the last tournament myself, and placed very respectably. But Steffen got antsy at the sight of all the golf clubs and balls, calling them "thinly disguised cudgels and projectile weapons," so I promised to send the email. Steffen's not always easy to deal with, but he's one of my favorite people.

Hitting Send, I look up and do a double take. Speak of the devil... though it's not actually Steffen, it's his twin brother who I didn't even know existed until a few years ago. I tried to find out what was up with that but very quickly hit a wall of silence that, in my experience, means something's classified. As the receptionist at the Dragon-Elf Alliance, and prior to that the Keeper of Time for the King of the Elves— same thing, different name—I'm great at recognizing the difference between "don't want to say" and "can't say because it's classified."

I smile and say, "Ronan, right? Brandt said you were coming in. Take a seat and I'll let him know you're here." I can see *him* out of the corner of my eye, but I refuse to acknowledge his presence. It's the first time he's been in the office all week, and I've been waiting for this chance to show him how pissed I am.

"Thank you." Ronan's voice is hoarse, but he clears his throat and smiles back at me. I blink, disconcerted. His face is identical to Steffen's, and Steffen never smiles.

As Ronan turns away, Eoin glares suspiciously at his back, and indignation mixes with my simmering anger. How dare he stand there with his arms crossed, all judgy of someone Brandt personally introduced to me? Does he think he knows better than Brandt? How dare he even breathe the same air as me after what he did?

I snap, "What's your problem? Stop loitering in my space and go pretend you do some work around here."

Eoin's brow rises, but he doesn't say anything. Or leave, damn him.

"Ugh!" I throw up my hands in exasperation, then grab the spray bottle of water I keep on the desk and give him a few good spritzes. It's incredibly satisfying.

"Hey!" Eoin steps back fast, hands up in defense against the water. "Quit that!"

"Serves you right. Now get the mop and clean up that mess, then get to work," I order. He knows I'll spray him again if he doesn't, but this time with the other bottle. The one with the bespelled water that will make him itch for the rest of the day. I may not be as big and muscled as a lot of the people here, but I know how to maintain order in the office. Eoin knows the regular bottle was the only warning he'll get.

He gives me a flat look, but fetches the mop from the

utility closet and swabs the wet spot on the floor. I keep one eye on him but pretend he doesn't exist.

The security gate opens, and Steffen steps out. Ronan, who I'd forgotten was here, goes to meet him. Seeing them together is a little trippy—the clothes and hair are the only way to tell them apart, unless you count Steffen's scowl.

Ronan smiles at me again, then follows Steffen through the security gate, and I focus all my attention on the screen in front of me. I am alone. There is nobody else here. Certainly not a six-foot-tall warrior hottie who smashed my heart to pieces.

Okay, not my heart. Nobody who's heard the stories of Eoin's past could think their heart would be safe with him. Eoin's known for being a good time, not a long time, and I'd never get into anything with him expecting a commitment.

But definitely my pride was smashed. My ego. My weekly budget. Manscaping and new clothes for a hot date are expensive, and the price doesn't change just because the date turns out to be not-so-hot.

From the corner of my eye, I see *nobody* put the mop away and come to stand beside my desk. I pretend to be reading an email. Dammit, why won't the phone ring? The thing never fucking stops when there's a bunch of people waiting, but right now, when I would desperately welcome all four lines lighting up, it's silent.

"Dáithí..." He pitches his voice low, coaxing. Or he would if he existed. Which he *does not*. "Come on, Dáithí. You can't just ignore me forever."

If he really believes that, he's got a very rude awakening coming his way. Sure, I can't ignore him professionally, but that doesn't mean I have to chat with him. I'll put through calls and coordinate visitors and do all the other things I take care of for everyone in the office, but that's it. No more special coffee orders, no more flirty notes, no more favors. He has a weakness for Double-Stuff Oreos, but I'm no longer ordering them for the break room. It's back to the boring cookies.

"Dáithí, please. Just let me explain. How can I explain when you won't even look at me?"

The nerve! I turn on him. "Explain? Explain?!" My voice rises. "There is no explaining!"

"I swear there is," he pleads, looking at me with those big, chocolate-colored eyes that used to give me butterflies but don't anymore. Nope. Nuh-uh. "Please? I'm so sorry, but I swear, there's an explanation."

I sniff. "Oh, really? You can *explain*, can you? Go on, then."

He blinks. "Really?"

"Sure." I shrug. "Explain why you flirted with me, made me think you were interested. Why you asked me out and promised me a good time. Why I turned up to the restaurant"—after many preparations—"and found you'd pre-ordered an expensive bottle of wine and hors d'oeuvres for us... but you weren't there. You never showed. And you stuck me with the check!" That's the part that burns the most. I was excited when I arrived and found he'd gone to such trouble. I accepted a glass of wine and waited, sure he'd be there any minute... any second now... surely he was about to walk in the door? I even tried calling, convinced he must be on his way, stuck in traffic. But he never showed, and eventually, humiliated and infuriated by the pitying looks from other diners and the servers, I got up to leave.

Only for the manager to cringe as she presented me with the bill. Another expense my budget wasn't prepared for. At least she had the heart to let me take the bottle of wine and hors d'oeuvres with me. She even slipped in a big slice of chocolate mousse cake for me to eat at home, in my underwear, alone, between swigs of rich red wine that cost more than I usually spend on a whole meal.

"They charged you?" In his defense—*no, Dáithí, no defense!* —he sounds outraged. "They made me leave a credit card on file! I thought... I am *so* sorry. I'll pay you back. How much was it?" He's already reaching for his wallet.

The figure I name is double what it actually cost, and he pauses, shooting me a suspicious look, but then hands over the cash anyway. I guess he feels guilty. I can live with that—I got my balls waxed, and he didn't bother to turn up.

"I swear, I would have been there if I could," he says earnestly, putting his wallet away.

"Got kidnapped, did you? Locked in someone's basement?" I look him up and down. "Pity they didn't keep you for a while longer. Maybe hit you with a pipe a few times."

There's a sharp inhalation, and we both spin to see a wide-eyed woman in a business suit standing on the other side of the reception desk. I didn't even hear her come in.

"Good morning," I greet with a professional smile. "Welcome to the DEA. How can I help you today?"

She looks from me to Eoin and back again. I think she's a shifter, but she could be a succubus. Sometimes I can't tell right away. "I... uh... I don't want to interrupt."

I wave off her concern. "Oh, don't worry about him. He was just about to explain why he led me on, asked me out, and then stood me up at a fancy restaurant."

Her eyes narrow. "Forget the pipe, someone needs to hit him with a car."

Shifter, then. Probably a hellhound. They tend to overreact. Eoin clears his throat uncomfortably.

"I bought new clothes and everything," I tell her, and because she's clearly on my wavelength, she instantly understands what "everything" entails.

"Oh, honey," she commiserates. "A man like that is *not* worth your time. No matter how pretty he looks, you can do so much better. I have some cousins with good jobs and all their hair—they'd bow down and worship me if I set them up with a guy like you."

I bask in the compliment—and a little in Eoin's growl. *That's right, buddy—I have* options. *I am a hot commodity.*

"That's so sweet of you. Stop by on your way out, and I'll make sure you have my number," I promise. "But for now, I don't want to make you late."

She smirks at Eoin—who glowers back—before saying, "I have an appointment with Maire in accounting."

"Let me just— Oh, here she is." I take my finger off the switchboard as Maire comes through the security gate.

"I thought you might be chatting to Dáithí," she says. "He's so easy to talk to, isn't he?"

"A complete delight," my new friend agrees, and I smile at them both. I *am* delightful.

They go off toward the meeting rooms, and I turn back to Eoin. "You were saying how you were chained up by a madman and beaten with a pipe."

A tiny smile teases his lips. "Not quite. I got called to work."

I wait, but that seems to be it. "You got called to work."

"Yes."

"And a dog ate your phone so you couldn't call me? And then it ate all the phones of everyone on your team, so you couldn't borrow one?" I understand that being in charge of the king's personal security is complicated, and I know he often gets called in unexpectedly. I've seen him and others on his team coming back into the office after leaving for the day, or I've gotten here in the morning and found them straggling in after an emergency kept them busy all night. It's part of why I keep the break room so well-stocked. If he'd called to tell me he had to work and needed a rain check, it would have been fine. Disappointing, sure, but I would have just changed clothes and ordered takeout. After all, despite all the flirting and sweet words, it's not like I expected this to turn into anything more than a few hot nights.

Leaving me sitting at the restaurant, though? Not okay.

"I couldn't." He grimaces. "It sounds like I'm making excuses, but I swear, Dáithí, I'm not. There are times when we get a call and immediately have to go offline. If I'd already been with you when the call came, I would have had to leave without explaining why. It doesn't happen a lot, but it does happen sometimes. It was just shitty luck that Saturday was one of those times." He runs his hand through his silky dark hair. He cut it super short not long after we moved here, but that didn't last long. Since then, it's been a gorgeous, touchable chin-length. "I couldn't even tell you this much until today."

I eye his repentant, pleading expression. He seems genuine. And fuck knows, I want to relent and give him another chance, *if* he's telling the truth.

"You know there are ways for me to check on this story? I have sources."

He nods. "I know. And I fully expect you to. If you need time to think about it, I'm okay with that. But please, please believe there is no way I would ever have stood you up if I didn't have to." He leans forward. "I've been waiting months to taste you. I'm *starving* for you."

Well, now. That's more like it.

"Get to work. I need to think this over."

"But you believe me?"

"I believe that I'm going to ask around and confirm your story."

"Dáithí—"

I pick up the *other* water bottle, the red one. Usually I only need to use it on dragons, who forget this is a profesional government office and think they can get around my warnings. Elves aren't delusional like that, and Eoin backs away with his hands up.

"Okay, I'm going. Take all the time you need."

I watch him walk away—because who could resist—and when he reaches the security gate, he glances back, catching me.

The bastard winks. "Take as much time as you need," he repeats, "to think of me. *All* of me."

Well played.

As he disappears into the office proper, I take a minute to send some sneaky messages, feeling people out about what happened on Saturday.

By noon, I'm convinced that he was telling the truth.

And then, late in the afternoon, a courier arrives. "Delivery for... uh... D-Da..."

I take pity on the poor human kid and glance at the clipboard he thrusts toward me. "Oh, that's me. It's Dáithí."

"Dory?"

"No. But thanks for trying." I've been assured there are people on Earth who *do* know how to pronounce my name, but if they live in this country, I've yet to find one.

The boy slinks away, and I regard the glittery gold gift bag he left behind. Red tissue paper is exploding from the top in a luxurious froth. There's a little white envelope dangling from one handle, and I tug it free and pull out the card.

Dáithí—

Last week I heard you say you'd kiss a cock-roach if it would bring you chocolate. Put these on my account. I look forward to feeding them to you one by one.

Eoin

A grin spreads across my face. Well, now. A man who listens to the important things.

Inside the bag, I find a box from the gourmet chocolatier two blocks away, the one I can't afford. Definitely not for a dozen gorgeous truffles that are begging me to take a bite.

I pop one into my mouth and moan as the chocolate melts on my tongue, my tastebuds flooded with hints of cinnamon and rum. Okay. A man who grovels like this might deserve a second chance. Especially since it wasn't really his fault he fucked up in the first place. I grab my phone, take a photo of the chocolates with one missing, and send it to him.

Your account has been opened.

CHAPTER TWO

Eoin

PRESENT—AUGUST

IF MY YOUNGER SELF COULD SEE ME now, he'd sprain a rib laughing. Or want to know if I'd suffered some kind of traumatic brain injury. What other reason could there be for me to be stressed over my situationship not being a relationship, as my friend Hagen just said. Only the fact that we're at work keeps me from ripping off one of his arms. I'm not usually a violent person—in my profession, a clear head and deliberate actions are best—but said profession has given me a lot of knowledge and skills that would help in the arm-ripping department.

"Don't call it that" is all I say. "Why are you here, again?" He has his own office down the hall, where he and the other operations rollout people manage infrastructure and resourcing for dragon and elf enclaves around the world. We've mostly integrated with humans and the community of species in their existing cities, but we have some specific needs that the native inhabitants of this planet don't, and it's Hagen's job to manage that. If I didn't know he'd been doing it successfully for thousands of years, I'd worry about putting such an important task in the hands of such a feckless dragon.

"I'm here because when I went to pick up a package at reception, I heard the delivery guy ask Dáithí if he's seeing anyone, and Dáithí said 'Not really.' Come the fuck on, man. You gotta step up."

Ouch. I knew Dáithí didn't consider me his boyfriend, despite the many, many, *many* hints I've dropped about making it official, but knowing he still considers himself to be pretty much single is a punch to the gut.

"Mind your own business" is all I can think to say. I wasn't expecting to have to defend my... situationship today.

Ugh. That word is awful.

"Yeah, that's not gonna happen." Hagen plants his ass on the corner of my desk. "So, I'll ask again, why are you in a situationship and not a relationship?"

I glance around the office, hoping one of my team will rescue me, but they're mostly staring studiously at their screens, pretending not to listen. Ari, on the other hand, is kicked back in his chair, watching avidly. He's such a gossip whore.

"What does that even mean, anyway? Situationship." I spit the word like it tastes bad. Which it does, since it implies that Dáithí and I aren't in a committed, happy relationship.

"It means what you and Dáithí are doing now, where you act like a couple and fuck like a couple, but won't own up to the fact that you *are* a couple."

Yeah, that sums it up. "You're not going to let this go, are you?"

"Nope!"

"Even though we're at work and both have important things to do?"

Hagen scoffs. "Dude, please. Our bosses are the king

and *Brandt*. I can guarantee you that if I asked the wing-leader of all dragons if I could ask you about this during work hours, he'd be in here himself, waiting for you to spill the tea."

I can't dispute that. Dragons don't make the most formal of bosses.

"But—"

"If you like," Ari interrupts, a thread of laughter in his voice, "I can go across the hall and ask the king if it's okay. He might want us to wait until he can get Jared on the phone to listen in, though."

There's a rustle of coughs and stifled chuckles from the rest of the team, and I aim my glare around the room. "I hate you all." Ari's right, though. Both the king and his new consort have hinted about me and Dáithí more than once. Jared and Dáithí have formed a friendship, but it hasn't helped me any. Probably because Jared hates me.

"Now that we've established that we're in the right and you hate us," Hagen says in that annoyingly cheerful way only dragons can pull off, "talk. Why haven't you and Dáithí made it official?"

I grit my teeth. This isn't humiliating at all. "He doesn't want to."

In hindsight, I should have recorded this moment. It's not often I get to shock a dragon speechless.

"Say what?" Hagen manages at last.

"He doesn't think I'm commitment material." Every word makes me hate my past self, because it's true that there's a lot of evidence to support his belief. "Anytime I even hint that we might be boyfriends or that I want to be, he shoots me down. Says he doesn't expect that from me, that he knows I don't have it in me to give." That last sentence rubs my throat raw. Maybe once I wasn't a commitment kind of person, but I'm older now—and more importantly, I'm with Dáithí now. I don't want anyone else, can never imagine wanting anyone else. Just him.

"Yikes." All traces of levity are gone from Hagen as he pats me on the shoulder. "I'm sorry, bro. That sucks hard."

The sympathy, as much as it stings my pride, soothes the part of me that's felt so reje—

"Okay!" Hagen's on his feet, clapping his hands. I don't know why, but I recognize that look on his face, and it doesn't bode well for me. "We have a very important project here, people."

Oh, no. Sliding down in my chair, I stare at the phone and will it to ring. I don't even care who's on the other end of the line, as long as they give me a reason to leave.

"There's not much we can do," Brayan says, giving up on the whole "not listening" farce. "Dáithí's got the right to decide who he wants to be in a relationship with, and we can't change Eoin's past."

"It would take too long to even try," Hagen agrees.

"Hey!" I straighten. "It wasn't that bad."

Huh. The way all nine people in the office look at me skeptically is so perfectly executed, I almost think they practiced.

"It wasn't," I protest. "I never lied to anyone or made them think I wanted more than I did. And I sure as fuck never asked anyone for a commitment. The fact that I am now should be enough to prove I've changed." Dammit. Why can't Dáithí trust that?

"He's got a point," someone says, but I'm not paying attention. My brain has locked on to that one question: Why *can't* Dáithí trust that?

"Do you think he's just not interested?" I blurt, feeling ill at the thought. "Is... Am I just someone to kill time with while he waits for someone he actually cares about?"

The tiny pause before anyone replies is all it takes for my

mouth to fill with bile. Then nine voices burst out with protests that *of course* Dáithí cares about me.

Somehow, I'm not convinced.

"You've been together for over a year," Ari points out. "If he was just killing time, he'd have moved on by now. It's not like he doesn't have other options."

The reminder that Dáithí's too good for me isn't what I wanted to hear, but it's somehow comforting. He *does* have other options. He's cute and clever, and everyone who wanders into his orbit falls under the spell of his charm. It's impossible not to like Dáithí, and I know he gets hit on all the time.

My bruised heart picks itself up and prepares to go another round. "That's true. It doesn't help much, but it's true."

"Hmm." Hagen leans his hip against my desk. I'm just glad he's not sitting on it again. "Interesting. He doesn't want to be single or date other people— Wait. You're exclusive, right? I just assumed..."

I press my hand to the bottom of my ribs, where it feels like some kind of fire monster is trying to claw its way out. The thought of Dáithí with someone else is horrendous. "We're exclusive." It's something we agreed on from the outset, that neither of us would see other people without letting the other know. Dáithí suggested it in response to the first time I asked if we were officially together. Not what I'd thought he was going to say.

"Okay, so if he's been committed to not seeing other people for over a year, why won't he commit to being officially with you? That doesn't make sense." He shakes his head. "There's more going on."

Since this whole conversation hasn't done anything to change the situation but *has* succeeded in not just reminding me how shitty I feel about the whole thing but also making my personal life fodder for gossip among my subordinates—not to mention pity. Gotta love when the people you manage feel sorry for you—I'm pretty much ready to have done with it all.

"Whatever's going on, I'll deal with it. In the meantime, we all have work to do, so it's time for you to go." I put all the authority of my job into my voice. It doesn't work all that well on Hagen, since he doesn't report to me and also used to be my roommate. If I couldn't make him leave my stuff alone, there's no way he'll abandon a juicy puzzle about someone's love life. He lives for stuff like this.

"Don't worry," he assures me. "We'll fix this. Get ready to wave your situationship goodbye and say hello to commitment!"

What a disturbing promise. My gaze tracks him out to the hallway, and horror floods me at the sight of King Raðulfr standing in his office doorway, Brandt beside him, both of them clearly having overheard what Hagen said. The king looks mildly sympathetic—he knows a bit about the issue, since it's hard to resist when my species leader offers a listening ear—but Brandt's expression is pure, avid curiosity.

Sighing, I get up and go to intercept. The king's office is a more private place for this conversation than the security office or the hallway.

"You're in a situationship?" Brandt asks before I even reach them. "And do you want to keep it or not?"

The king rolls his eyes. "Inside," he orders, tugging Brandt away from the door so I can join them. I wait until the door is firmly closed before answering.

"Dáithí has some concerns about a committed relationship with me," I say simply. "I'm trying to convince him that I'm a good bet. That's all. Except that I think we'd both prefer not to be office gossip."

The king winces, and Brandt waves that off dismissively.

"Too late. Everyone knows something's going on with you two. I hadn't heard that Dáithí has cold feet, though. The rumors all suggest that you're the one holding back."

"Fuck," I whisper, then remember who I'm talking to. "I beg your pardon, I—"

"No, fuck sums it up pretty well," Brandt agrees, and the king nods.

"It does. I'm so sorry, Eoin. I hadn't heard that particular rumor, or I would have made you aware."

Brandt turns on him. "You mean you knew about this?"

"Eoin confided some of his concerns to me, yes. And I kept them to myself, because that's the respectful thing to do." His tone is heavy with meaning.

Sighing, Brandt says, "Yeah, yeah. I can keep a secret." He narrows his eyes at me. "Although... now that I know the truth, I could be helpful. Dáithí's never been a commitment-shy person. Why would he suddenly become one with you?"

Does everyone in this building want to rub salt in that particular wound?

"That's a question that haunts my nightmares. Please don't try to help. This is something Dáithí and I will sort out in our own time." I hope.

And if not, then I'll just be his situationship for as long as he'll have me.

CHAPTER THREE

Dáithí

"No." I don't even bother to glare at the miscreant who dares to ask a favor of me after such a vile insult.

"Please, Dáithí," Niamh begs. "I'm sorry. You know I'm sorry. I didn't mean it—I don't think that way! But I was—"

"Excuses aren't welcome here," I say icily. "If you'll step out of the way, there are people waiting."

Her face screws up in frustration, but she steps aside, probably not willing to risk annoying me any further. I'll forgive her eventually, but we elves live a very long time, so that's not likely to help with her current problem.

The elf who was waiting behind her has a wary expression on his face. I don't recognize him, and I know everyone who works here, so he's probably questioning our professionalism. That's how I know he's never had to work on reception before—if he had, he'd recognize that I'm just doing what I must to keep the office running. We receptionists are a rare combination of protector, assistant, and parent.

I smile. "Welcome to the DEA. How can I help you?"

He pulls his attention away from Niamh, who's hovering pitifully a few feet away, and steps forward. "Hi. I have an appointment with Caolan. I'm Erik, from the Warhammers Hockey Club."

The what now? Why does someone from a hockey club have an appointment with Caolan? "I didn't know there were any elves involved with the team," I comment as I bring up the visitor list. Yep, there he is: Erik, Warhammers HC. The notes link to the meeting room booking under Caolan's name. I click on that while Erik explains earnestly that he works in the marketing department and he's hoping the sport can be another way for elves to integrate with the other community species. It would be very sweet if I had any interest in sports beyond the athletes.

The meeting invitation shows that the king and Eoin are attending too, which is interesting. I guess the king is planning to get involved in the sport? After what happened when he took Jared to a game last season, that's a little surprising.

"Have a seat, and Caolan will be right out," I tell Erik, sending Caolan a message that his visitor is here.

Erik wanders over to the waiting area, and I grab my phone and send a text to Eoin.

Is the king going to sponsor a hockey team?

There's got to be *some* benefit—aside from the phenomenal sex—to risking my emotional stability with Eoin. If I can't get the occasional bit of non-classified insider information from him, what's the point?

I'm not stupid. I know a lot of people are wondering what's going on with us. We've been "seeing" each other for about eighteen months now, and while that's not a long time for a species as long-lived as ours, it's a long time to just be casually dating. Especially since neither of us is seeing anyone else, and we spend more time together than most people who are keeping it casual. Casual daters probably don't keep clothes at each other's homes.

But that's all it can be. I'm already too invested as it is, and I can't afford to put more of myself into this. Eoin called me his boyfriend once, and even though it hurt me to do it, I shut that down as fast as I could. The only reason I let myself get into this with Eoin, of all people, was because I knew he'd never want more than friendship and sex. That's all I want. I like Eoin—of course I do. I'm very fond of him, to quote everyone on *Downton Abbey* who seems incapable of expressing emotions in public. And what we do together in bed is exceptional. But I don't need the heartbreak of a relationship that's doomed to fail, and he's notorious for not wanting relationships at all. That's why I let my thing with Eoin grow beyond the couple of nights I originally thought it would be—because I knew he'd never want me to risk my heart on him.

Only, lately it's seemed like maybe he wants to try something different from his usual commitment-phobic ways. If I have to say goodbye to what we have, I will.

I have to muffle a grunt as my stomach cramps *hard*. For no reason. Absolutely none.

My phone makes a whooshing sound as Eoin replies.

> Does that mean the rep from the team is here? Not sponsor. Maybe get involved somehow. Jared likes hockey.

Caolan comes out through the security gate, shooting me a little wave before he goes to collect Erik and usher him toward the meeting rooms. I wave back. Caolan and I have worked together for a long time, and I've always liked him, but more so since we've come to Earth. His boyfriend and new friends have brought out a side of him that's a lot of fun.

"Dáithí," Niamh murmurs tentatively, distracting me from my thoughts. I narrow my eyes at her.

"I already said no."

She makes pitiful eyes at me, but I'm resolute. If I give in now, everyone will think they can walk all over me.

The security gate opens again, and this time it's Eoin and the king who walk through, obviously on their way to the hockey meeting. I acknowledge them with a smile and nod, and the king calls a greeting. He's very respectful of everyone who works here.

Eoin winks at me, then catches sight of Niamh and frowns. He murmurs something to the king, who nods and continues into the hallway. Eoin changes direction to join me and my latest nemesis at the reception desk.

"Good morning, Dáithí," he says, his voice warm with that special note he only directs at me... these days, anyway.

"Good morning," I reply cheerfully, as if he didn't wake up in my bed and drive me to work today.

"Are you having a good day so far?"

I consider it carefully. "Pretty good, yes. Not quite as good as it would have been if you'd told me about this hockey... thing." He knows how much I love gossip. That's why I'm still working reception after all these years, even though I've been offered a place on Caolan's team multiple times. People talk to me more in this job than they would if they thought I had seniority.

"I apologize for that oversight. Caolan only told me about it yesterday, and since then I've been... distracted." He flashes a wicked grin to remind me I'm the reason for said distraction.

"I guess I can forgive you, this one time. You'll take me to lunch to make up for it, won't you?" And fill me in on how the meeting went and what's been decided.

He nods. "Of course. One o'clock?"

That's when one of the assistants from the administration team usually comes to cover the desk so I can have my break. Nobody mentioned a change of plans today, so I agree.

"One's perfect."

"Wonderful. Now... is there a reason Niamh's standing here with a look on her face like her beloved pet went missing?"

"She doesn't have a pet," I inform him. That's the kind of thing I know about people. "But there *is* a reason. It's because she's hoping I'll feel sorry for her."

"I see." He turns to Niamh. "Anything to add that I, your direct supervisor, might need to know? Since you're clearly not getting any work done standing here."

Judging by the look on Niamh's face, she'd rather continue to beg me than tell her boss—who's sleeping with me—about her unprofessional behavior. It almost makes me feel bad for her.

Finally she sighs, lifts her chin, and looks Eoin directly in the eye. "My meeting room privileges were revoked, and I'm trying to convince Dáithí to lift the ban."

Eoin's brows draw together, making him look all smart and hot, like he's thinking about important things. I wonder how he'd feel about wearing a pair of wire-rimmed glasses? Just when we're alone. He can put them on and think about serious stuff while I spin some wild fantasies for my spank bank, which I'll need one day when this thing between us is over.

"Why were your privileges revoked?"

I rest my chin in my palm and wait for her to answer.

"I left a mess." Niamh's gaze isn't quite as steady now, and I can tell Eoin has noticed.

"Niamh," he says, his voice taking on his "head of security" tone, "you're not a child, I'm not your parent, and trickling the information out in this way is keeping both of us from our jobs. Please explain the entire situation so we can find a resolution and move on."

Surprisingly, that seems to help Niamh find her backbone. "I left a mess in a meeting room after I used it," she says clearly. "More than once. Dáithí asked me a few times to make sure the room was in the same condition when I left as it was when I arrived, but I... didn't. Last week, I left a room untidy again, and when Dáithí came to speak to me about it, I was... I was rude to him."

Eoin's jaw tightens, and his eyes narrow as he thinks it through. The DEAs shared space policy allows me to suspend meeting room privileges for anyone who doesn't respect the rules around their use, one of which is to clean up after yourself. Niamh broke the rules, I tried to give her some leeway, but when she proved to be a repeat offender, I suspended her privileges. It's all above-board, per policy, and Eoin's input isn't needed, even if he is her supervisor. He knows that.

But Niamh just admitted to being rude to me, the man he's dating, and his inner protector doesn't like that. For a moment, he struggles with it—the need to defend me and avenge my honor or whatever, versus the knowledge that there's no reasonable need for him to step in at all.

Finally, reason and professionalism win out—possibly along with the memory of what happened last time he tried to leap to my rescue when I had everything perfectly under control. "I'll leave you to it, then. See you at one, Dáithí."

"Bye," I reply cheerfully.

We both wait until he's into the hallway and unlikely to hear us, and then Niamh says, "I'm definitely getting a week of crappy jobs."

"Probably." If I don't want Eoin interfering with what

happens in my domain, I can't interfere with what happens in his... even if they're directly connected.

She sighs. "I really am sorry. I know your job is so much more complex than answering phones and tidying up—if I had to deal with all the people you do, I'd have quit long ago."

"Thank you. You're still suspended for another two weeks, though. And after that, if the messes keep happening, I'll make it permanent."

With a grimace and a nod, she concedes, "I guess that's reasonable." Flipping her hand in a wave, she wanders back toward her desk, leaving me with a second to myself.

I grab my phone and send a text to Jared, the king's new consort. Though, does five months count as new? Whatever. He and I are sort-of friends, and since supposedly he's the hockey fan, he might be able to share some news.

> Aww, the king's getting involved with hockey to impress you!

There. It shouldn't take him too long to respond—he's still technically on summer break from teaching for a few more weeks, and he doesn't have any official consort duties or appearances scheduled for today.

My phone chimes a moment later.

> Yeah, aren't I lucky?

How sweet, but not forthcoming. Now, what's the best way to get more information?

Before I can start typing again, he sends another message.

> That's what boyfriends do. Doesn't it make you wish you had one?

I drop my phone on the desk, as though that will make

the pointed question go away. Damn him. One slightly vulnerable conversation, months ago, and he now knows more about my feelings than anyone else. I only said so much because he was so unsure of himself back then. Sometimes friends are the worst.

CHAPTER FOUR

Eoin

I'M NOT sure what happened between me going to my meeting and lunch, but something upset Dáithí. He wasn't his usual self while we were eating—didn't even ask about the meeting with the hockey club—and six hours later, he still seems off. Niamh swears that he was fine when she left, that they'd worked out their differences. I'm not totally convinced. She might just be saying it because she wants me to forget she was rude to him.

I don't think I'm a bad boss, or a bad person, but sometimes it's hard to hold back the part of me that wants to drape Dáithí in silk, install him on a velvet chaise, and protect him from life while I brush his hair and feed him chocolate truffles. That part of me is very unhappy with Niamh right now.

"Did everything go okay with Niamh today?" I ask casually as I join him on the couch. We're at my place tonight, because Dáithí says I have the better TV to watch whatever his latest reality show obsession is. I wasn't about to argue—given how withdrawn he was at lunch, I was half expecting tonight to be one of the ones where he insists we be apart.

"Yeah, it was fine. You don't need to be mad at her on my behalf."

He doesn't sound annoyed, but I can't shake the feeling that something's not right with him, so I say, "I know you can take care of yourself. I'm still mad at her, but I'm not going to interfere."

That wins me a smile. "Aw. You're learning." He pats my thigh, but when he turns back to the TV, his hand slides away —and so does the smile.

Shit. How can I make this better? What even is this?

I hesitate for a few seconds longer, then throw caution to the wind. "Is everything okay? You seem... preoccupied."

Dáithí goes still, then sighs. That can't be good.

My fears are confirmed when he mutes his show and half turns toward me, tucking his leg up on the seat of the couch.

"I think..." He stops, and I stay quiet. I'm not completely sure what he wants to say, but every one of my instincts is screaming that I'm not going to like it. "Do people think they have the right to tell you their opinion of your personal life?"

I blink a few times, processing the question. It's not what I expected him to say. I feel like I might be getting a reprieve but I'm not out of the woods yet. "Sometimes," I admit, remembering the way Hagen cornered me the other day. "Usually they're close friends, and I tell them where they can stick their opinions."

He sighs again. "Yeah. That's normally how I handle it too." For what feels like eternity, he stares into space, his face pensive. This is really bothering him. Maybe it's not about me, after all? I assumed that someone had lectured him about our "situationship"—damn Hagen for getting that word stuck in my head—but it could be something else.

"Is it something I could help with?" I ask impulsively, drawing his attention back to me.

His expression softens into one I'll never get sick of being on the receiving end of—fond caring. Dáithí might be holding back from a commitment, but I don't have any doubt that he cares about me.

Then fondness morphs into unwilling determination. "I think it's time for us to end this."

It's funny, I always assumed that if this moment came, I'd feel awful. Like I couldn't breathe or was going to throw up. I assumed I'd be overtaken with anxiety and fear, maybe even cry.

Instead, my emotions blank out completely, my mind clearing as adrenaline pumps through my system. I know what this is—I've felt this before. My body is ready for battle. I'd laugh, if I wasn't facing the most important battle of my life.

"Why?" I ask, and even my voice sounds normal. Steady, and a little curious. Not a quaver in sight.

It's Dáithí's turn to blink in surprise. "I... What do you mean, why? I don't need to have a reason!"

I shrug. "Of course you don't, and if you really want to end things, that's your prerogative. I just wondered if this is *your* decision or if someone else has bullied you into it with their opinions."

His mouth drops open. "Nobody *bullied* me! I don't get bullied, thank you. I'm perfectly capable of handling bullies and everyone else when they try to shove their opinions down my throat."

"That's what I always believed," I agree. "If you're telling me this has nothing to do with what anyone else thinks, I'll accept that. I'm confused, though, because this morning our arrangement"—there's the slightest hitch on that word, but I power on, hoping he won't notice—"suited us both fine. We like each other's company, and I know I'm not being presumptuous when I say we're like fire in bed."

The corner of Dáithí's mouth turns up as his gaze heats,

hopefully with the memory of what we did last night. "Yeah," he breathes.

I spread my hands in a "there you go" gesture. "So it seems odd to me that everything was good, but now it isn't, and somewhere in between then and now people have been mouthing off."

Dáithí stares at me, then shakes his head. "You're good."

My heart is beating fast, thanks to the adrenaline, but I'm still in control of my feelings. "Am I? I thought *we* were good. That our arrangement was good."

"It is, but..."

It takes every ounce of willpower I have not to interrupt. Not to tell him to forget the buts. If I do that, he'll see through my calm façade and this will all be over.

"I know you want more, Eoin."

Or he could have already seen through my façade. Fuck. What do I say now that can stop this from turning into a disaster? "I've lived long enough to know that I'm not always going to get everything I want. Besides, wanting more doesn't mean I'm not already happy with what I have."

He's not convinced. "It's cruel of me—"

"If the rest of that sentence is about me, don't bother finishing it," I cut in. "Nobody's forcing me to be here, Dáithí. If I don't have a problem with our current arrangement, then why should anyone else? You and I are the only ones who get a say."

"Yeah."

Relief surges through me—

"You and I are the only ones who get a say," he continues, "and I can't keep... I don't know, leading you on like this. You want us to be boyfriends, and I can't believe that you're boyfriend material. It's wrong of me to keep you trapped in this weird pre-relationship limbo just because I like your company and you fuck like it's your life's purpose."

My cock twitches with pride, but the rest of me is frantically trying to regroup. He's really ending it, dammit. What am I supposed to do? I will *not* accept defeat; I've been on too many battlefields to just give up because it looks like I'm losing.

I go on the attack. "Why can't you see me as boyfriend material?"

He's not expecting that. "Huh?"

"You're right, I do want to be your boyfriend. Partner. Significant other. Whatever label we prefer is good with me. I want to be in a committed relationship with you, and I want everyone to know it. But like you just said, you don't see me as boyfriend material. Why not?"

"I..." He grimaces and looks away. "Come on, Eoin, don't make me say it. I don't want to hurt you."

"I asked the question, Dáithí. I'm prepared for whatever answer you might give, and I'll decide if it hurts me or not."

With a big, unhappy sigh, he concedes, "Fine. I don't trust that you really want a commitment. You've got thousands of years of dating history that points to you being a short-term fun guy, and there's nothing wrong with that. You don't need to try to be different now."

"Are you saying I'm not capable of change? Yeah, I've had a... varied love life." Really varied, if I'm being honest. "But most of that happened when I was a soldier and had almost no stability in my life. Fuck, for the last few thousand years, we didn't even think we'd survive. I've got a steady job now, and a home that isn't going to cease to exist. Who's to say it's not time for me to settle down?"

"Who's to say it is?" he counters. "You might want to give it a shot, but the Earth species have an expression for situations like this: A leopard doesn't change its spots."

What the fuck? Is he comparing me to a felid shifter? That makes no sense. "What's that supposed to mean?"

Dáithí's smile is sad. "You can't change who you really are."

Fury rises in me, destroying the clarity of mind I was so proud of. "And who is it you think I am? Someone who's incapable of making a promise and keeping it? What do you think this past year has been, Dáithí? We said we'd be monogamous, and I have been, happily. Why do you think making things official between us would change that?"

"I'm not saying you'd break a promise." He grabs my hand, suddenly intense. "Believe me, Eoin, I'd never say that. You're one of the most honorable people I've ever met. That's why I'd never expect more from you. Don't you get it? Eventually, you'd realize a relationship isn't what you want, but if you'd made a promise like this, you'd try to ride it out anyway. It would be up to me to end things for both our sakes, and I'd rather do that now and still be friends than have my heart broken later." He stops suddenly, dropping my hand and looking away. "So... you understand, don't you? Why it's best that we..." Trailing off, he bites his lip.

My anger receded at some point during his passionate little speech, and now my brain is spinning through a thousand different ideas, trying to find the one that will change his mind. One thing is very clear to me: This isn't just about my feckless past. It's not that he thinks I don't have it in me to make a commitment, that I'll deliberately break his heart. Somehow, he's gotten the idea that I'm physically incapable of wanting him for the long-term, as though my feelings for him will wear off eventually. I can't quite make sense of it, but it doesn't seem like he actually wants to end things, only that he thinks he needs to in order to protect us both.

That's some fucked-up bullshit, as my Earth friends like to say.

"I can't predict the future," I begin, glad that my voice is calm again. He jumps a little, like he wasn't expecting me to speak.

"That's not what I mean," he protests. "Every relationship has a chance of ending, I know that. People change. But it would be stupid of me to go into something knowing that you'd need to change for it to have a chance."

Ouch. "I don't need to change for our relationship to have a chance. You're wrong about who I am, Dáithí, and I want the chance to prove that to you."

He shakes his head. "We're right back where we started. I can't—"

"Not by agreeing to make things official—not yet, anyway. Hear me out. You tell me what I can do to prove I'm not actually the serial dater my past points toward me being. You can ask me any question you like, talk to my friends, my family—I'll even give you the contact details of my past lovers, if you want. Plus, if there's a task or something that I can do to show you... Maybe I could plant a garden? That's a long-term commitment." I'm getting off track. "What I mean is, think about what you need from me that would make you feel secure in a relationship with me. There's no time limit on this, so if you do want me to plant a garden and look after it for as long as it survives, I will."

That gets me a chuckle, and I consider it a win.

"I don't know," he says, but I can see the indecision in his eyes. "Testing you like that doesn't seem fair."

"Maybe it's not, but we both need to be comfortable with this, Dáithí. You've been honest about your concerns, and I'm telling you I'm willing to do whatever it takes to relieve them."

He looks me in the face, searching for something—sincerity, perhaps?—and then nods. "Okay."

Yessss! "I have one more condition," I add, because

winning has always made me reckless, and why shouldn't I push my luck?

"Oh?"

"While you're thinking about how to test me, and for the duration of it, however long it is, we continue as we have been."

An incredulous laugh bursts from him. "Seriously? You want to hang out and have sex like nothing's different while I test if you measure up as commitment material?"

Damn, yes. He's already admitted that he likes my company and the way I fuck, and I need every advantage I can get. "Yes."

"You've got brass balls, Eoin." He's grinning now. "I've always liked that about you."

"Oh yeah?" I raise a brow, almost giddy with relief. "Care to demonstrate how much you like my balls?"

CHAPTER FIVE

Dáithí

IT'S PROBABLY a sign that I made the wrong decision, but I'm incredibly relieved by the change in subject. Sex with Eoin is something I can do. It's as easy and natural as breathing. Negotiating the possibility of a relationship I know deep down is doomed to fail? Incredibly hard and anxiety-inducing.

I sink back into the couch and give Eoin an arch look. "If I remember right, you owe me a hand job after the other night. I believe your words were, 'I'd give a million handies for a hot meal I don't have to cook.'"

He laughs and reaches for my zipper. "I did say that... and you delivered. Okay, then, just relax and let me 'handle' everything."

My snort is probably as unsexy as that joke. "There's not going to be anything to handle if you—ohhhh." His hand sliding into my pants changes my mind. I've never been with anyone before who could affect me like this with just one, relatively simple, touch. It doesn't matter how bad his jokes are, my body will always respond to him.

I obediently raise my hips so he can pull my jeans down a

little and tuck my underwear under my balls, giving him excellent access to my already hard-as-fuck dick.

"Hmm," he says, running his finger across the ridges. "We're going to need things a little more wet." His head bends, and the wet heat of his mouth engulfs me, sliding down, down... all the way. Eoin's lack of a gag reflex is *so* attractive.

He works the length of my cock with his tongue, and when he pulls off a moment later, it's plenty wet. The air in the room feels cold after Eoin's mouth, but only for a second before he wraps one big, strong hand around me and begins working me over with firm, twisting strokes. I alternate between watching his hand and his face. The little crease of intent concentration between his eyes is so sexy. I've seen it—

"Uhhhh, yeah," I moan, interrupting my own train of thought as his thumb toys with the spongy spot below the head. One side of his mouth quirks in a half smile, but he never takes his eyes off his task. He's focused like this when he's guarding the king—or in battle—and knowing he brings the same attention to getting me off, like I'm special and precious...

It would be so easy to want this to last forever.

He brings his other hand into play, sliding a finger down to tickle lightly over the taut skin of my balls, and when my breath catches, his gaze flashes up to meet mine.

What I see there makes me swallow hard. Lust, yes. Affection and teasing, of course. But something else... Something I can't bring myself to believe for fear of my heart shattering.

"I love your cock, Dáithí," he murmurs, the low timbre of his voice racing through me like a shiver. "Love how it feels in my hand. Love the taste. Love watching you come undone when I fuck you."

I didn't think I was that close, but Eoin's power over me

runs deeper than I knew, because those words, his eyes on me, are all it takes to send me over the edge. My head falls back and I spurt so hard, I think I might have blacked out.

When I open my eyes, Eoin's licking my cum off his hand, a soft smile on his face as he watches me.

"Nine hundred and ninety-nine thousand, nine hundred and ninety-nine to go," he says.

It takes me a moment to catch on, and then I laugh—or try to. That orgasm drained me completely. I hold out my hand to him.

"What?"

"I'm a limp noodle, but I want your dick. So take me to the bedroom, where I'll lie back in comfort and you can fuck my face."

I've never seen a man move that fast in my life.

I MANAGE to ignore the monumentally stupid decision I made right up until the morning busy wave is done, and then, when I finally have a few seconds alone, no phone ringing, no visitor needing to be checked in, no apologetic dragons begging me to unjam the printer... that's when reality crashes in on me.

What the fuck did I do?

Groaning, I smack my head against my desk, managing to catch the edge of my keyboard. That just makes it more painful, but unfortunately doesn't help at all. Sighing, I rub my forehead and invoke a small healing spell to prevent any bruising. That's the last thing I need to explain.

So, using the furniture to beat myself up didn't help... now what? What am I supposed to do? I promised Eoin I'd test him, and it's bad enough that I've been toying with both our emotions for so long already. I can't let him down by not following through. Even though I know the outcome is just going to hurt us both more.

Because no matter how much I want to keep Eoin forever, it would only make him miserable in the end.

Maybe this test idea is for the best. Eoin's stubbornly refusing to see the truth in the situation, and this might open his eyes to reality. After all, what does it matter if we ended it yesterday or wait a little while longer, until he admits the test has convinced him he wants out? Either way will be less painful than committing to a relationship that's doomed to fail.

And, as selfish as it is, I'll still get to keep him for a little while longer.

But what the fuck am I going to use for a test? How do you test capacity for a long-term commitment without actually making a commitment?

"Dáithí?"

Startled, I snap my head up. Antje, one of my printer-jamming dragons, is on the other side of the desk, watching me cautiously.

"Yes?"

She tilts her head, eyes narrowing on my face. "Are you okay?"

My spine snaps straight, and I pull myself together. I will *not* have rumors going around that something's wrong with me. The piranhas don't need to smell my blood in the water... or whatever it is that makes them circle. Or is that sharks?

"Of course I'm okay. Did you need something?"

"Only, you were staring into space and muttering to yourself. I had to say your name three times before you heard me."

"You're mistaken. What do you need?"

Antje frowns. "I'm mistaken? How can I be mistaken? I said your name three times, and you didn't even notice me." She's not annoyed, more confused. Probably wondering if she actually could be mistaken. I love dragons, but their brains work differently from the rest of us.

"Antje. Do you need anything?"

"Oh." She shakes her head as though dismissing a thought. "Yes, please. How do I make the printer copy this double-sided?" She holds up a piece of paper. "I did one copy to test, like you told me, but it only copied one side."

I swear, there is a conspiracy in this office to see who can drive me into a mental breakdown. Someone must have the master spreadsheet with all the odds and people's bets. I hope the pot is a big one, because when I find out who's in charge, I'm confiscating every cent.

"There are instructions on the wall," I remind her, not bothering to mention that we all had the exact same training on how to use the printer. We all came to Earth and learned to use the technology here at the same time, so the fact that half the people in the office are somehow incapable *has* to be a conspiracy. "Come on, I'll show you."

I walk her through the steps of using the tray feeder, point out the laminated step-by-step instructions taped to the wall, and wait to make sure she doesn't accidentally jam the printer again—or worse. I'm not sure how, but dragons can make the printer do things the repair techs swear are impossible.

"Thank you so much, Dáithí," she says when the last of her copies slides into the tray. She snatches them up and hugs the stack of paper to her chest. "You're the best. I knew asking you for help was smarter than trying to work it out myself. My wife always tells me it's okay to ask for help."

My irritation dissipates. Sure, people can be exasperating, but most of them are pretty amazing when it all comes down to it.

"She's right about that. Asking for help is—" I stop.

Maybe smacking my head against the desk did some damage to my brain after all. The solution is so simple.

"Dáithí?" Antje's giving me that concerned look again.

"I just remembered something I need to get done this morning," I say, and her frown is chased away by a smile.

"I won't keep you, then. Thank you!" She swipes herself through the security gate as I return to my desk and glance at the time. The lull will be over soon, replaced by the midmorning rush, but I have just enough time to make a call.

"Hi, Dáithí." Jared's greeting is cautious, and I remember that I never texted him back after his slightly pushy message about Eoin.

"Hi. Look, I don't have a lot of time to talk right now, but I need your help."

"Of course." The caution is immediately gone from his voice. "Are you okay? Do you need me to come there?"

I pause, the shaky-warm feeling in my chest a surprise and also something I want to savor. I've had a lot of friends throughout my lifetime, but the closest ones were lost to the anomalies—one by one, in a slow attrition that carved itself painfully into my soul. My dearest friends and family members were whittled away, in some cases leaving me as the only one who could truly say I knew them. I have other friends, and many friendly acquaintances, but it's been a long time since I asked anyone for help.

And even longer since they responded with zero hesitation, even without knowing what I needed of them.

I called Jared because he knows both me and Eoin, already has some knowledge of the situation, and is a reasonable, calm kind of person. But maybe he's also a closer friend to me than I thought.

"Dáithí?"

"I'm okay," I assure him. "Could we meet for lunch? I did a thing that I thought was stupid, but it might not be that stupid after all, but I'm still not sure how I'm going to follow through with it."

It's his turn to pause. "I have no idea what you're talking about."

I sigh. "I know."

"You did something stupid? Is this stupid like you're going to lose your job or end up in prison? Or stupid like your hair is green?"

Gasping, I lift my hand to my hair. "Bite your tongue. If I decided to dye my hair green, it would be the perfect shade to complement my skin tone and I'd look amazing."

"Your hair's not green, then," he concludes, and it sounds like he might be laughing at me.

"It's not. But I'm not going to prison either. This is... something in between." Screw it, there's no point in making him wait. "I need to come up with a commitment test for Eoin."

"A... Okay. Dáithí, testing your partner isn't—"

"It's not like that," I interrupt. "It was his idea. I said we should break it off—"

"You *what*?"

"Don't act like that's a surprise. I already told you it wasn't a real relationship and that it was going to end soon." It's not like I've been pretending to anyone that Eoin and I are actually boyfriends—that was all him. I've told everyone who asks that we're casual.

"You said that, but I didn't think it was true," Jared replies, confirming my long-held theory that no matter what you tell people, they believe whatever they want. "I figured it would just eventually turn into a solid commitment."

"I think Eoin did too. Realizing that was what convinced me to end it. I don't want to lead him on when I know it can't go anywhere."

"But why—"

"I don't want to be rude, but I haven't even got to the point yet, and I don't have a lot of time," I cut in. "Eoin insisted I tell him why I didn't think things would work, because he's a pushy bastard like that, and when I said it was because he's not a long-term commitment person, he insisted I come up with a test so he can prove that he is. So now I have to think of a test, and I need help."

"Wow. Um. Well, fuck." Jared seems to be at a loss for words, which is *not* helpful. "I have a lot of questions. Lunch, right? I'll be there."

Relief floods me. He'll help me work out what my next steps are. "Thank you. Let's meet at that sushi place with the homemade wasabi."

"Yeah, sounds good. Is it okay if I bring Noah? Only I was supposed to be having lunch with him. I can cancel on him if you prefer—this is more important."

"Noah Cage?" I think about it. Noah's a team administrator for CSG, but he works directly with the lucifer. He's also human, but probably the meanest human I've ever met. I've always admired the way he keeps his people in line. "Sure, he might be able to help. He strikes me as the kind of person who'd know how to test others."

"Then we'll see you at one," Jared promises, and we end the call.

By the end of the day, I'll have a plan. If only it wasn't one that meant an end to Eoin in my life.

CHAPTER SIX

Dáithí

I PICK up my glass and take a drink while Jared and Noah process the whole story. I didn't leave out many details, since they'll need all the information to help me come up with the right test for Eoin.

"You're one hundred percent sure that Eoin won't be happy in a relationship with you?" Jared asks, a sympathetic frown turning down the corners of his mouth.

"It's not me, specifically," I clarify. I don't have self-esteem issues for them to fix. "He's just not the kind of person who can commit. It might make him happy at first, but eventually that will change, and then we'll both be miserable."

"Is this, like, a polyamory thing?" Noah wonders. "Because that's got nothing to do with commitment."

I shake my head. "I considered that, but I really don't think it is. For one thing, Eoin's old enough and open-minded enough to have realized for himself if he was polyamorous. It's general knowledge that he's always upfront about what he's offering when he hooks up with people, whether for a night or a bit longer. I don't think he'd be suddenly secretive about being polyam. I definitely don't think he'd tell me he wanted a committed relationship and not mention that, especially since we agreed to be monogamous while we were seeing each other."

"Nah, that seems unlikely," Noah agrees.

"And it doesn't fit with Eoin's character," Jared adds. "I've gotten to know him pretty well, and he's not afraid of the truth. Even when you wish he would be. But," he continues before I can ask what truth Eoin shared that Jared wished he hadn't, "that just makes me wonder *why* you're so sure Eoin can't be happy in a long-term committed relationship. Isn't that up to him to decide?"

I roll my eyes. Here we go again. "Do you really think someone who's had the same approach to romantic connections for *thousands* of years, with not a single actual relationship in all that time, is suddenly going to want forever with one person? I have a great opinion of myself, but not even I think Eoin's whole outlook on commitment is going to change because of me. He might want something with me now, but it's not going to last, and I don't want to give him everything only to have my heart broken again. Not when I know better."

They exchange a glance, the kind that makes me think back over what I've said. No, it's all—

"Again?" Noah asks softly. "That sounds like you've been burned before."

Dammit. I really don't want to get into that. "Haven't we all? Unlike Eoin, I've been someone's boyfriend before—quite a few people."

Jared leans forward. "But is all of this"—he waves a hand to encompass our conversation and the whole situation—"because of a specific past boyfriend who broke your heart?"

The question stops me in my tracks. "No!" Is it? "No," I repeat firmly. "Maybe there's stuff that happened in the past that gives me some insight on situations like this, but the decisions I'm making are based on me and Eoin."

"Because Eoin's a commitment-phobe." Noah's watching me with an unreadable expression.

"Only when it comes to romantic relationships," I correct. "He's got no problem committing to long-term friendships, and before we came here and things changed, he was in the same job for longer than I've known him. That's the point. I've known Eoin for a very long time—more than fifty times longer than either of you has been alive. I knew of his reputation before that. It's not unreasonable of me to believe that after happily and willingly choosing to avoid relationships for that long, he's not going to change." I'm repeating myself now. Why doesn't anyone want to understand this?

"That's a fair point," Jared concedes, fiddling with his chopsticks. "I still think it's possible, though. People *do* change."

I shrug. There's no point in arguing about that. He's right, people do change sometimes, either because of life influences or because they want to. That doesn't mean Eoin will.

"I still want to hear about the guy who burned you," Noah says. "Maybe it's not directly impacting your decision, but you did say it gave you 'insight' on it."

Ugh. I'd forgotten that when you talk to friends about your life, they take it as an invitation to dig into everything. I love gossip, but not so much when I'm the one being talked about.

Still, I did invite them here, and I do need help. "There's not a lot to talk about," I admit. "It was a long time ago. I was very young and romantic, and Alan was a little older, very charming, and the local..." I search for the right word in English. It's been a long time since I used my translator spell, but sometimes I miss it. "...heartthrob, I guess. His reputation was a lot like Eoin's, though in hindsight, he wasn't always so upfront about only wanting a good time. There were a few broken hearts in his wake."

"Did he lie to get you to sleep with him?" Jared asks fiercely.

"If he did, tell me his last name. I have some friends who'd like to meet him," Noah adds.

I grin and wave them off. "Not me, but I think he might have to some others. And he's gone—I heard years later that he tripped while drunk and impaled himself on a fence paling. Dead before anyone knew, much less could try to heal him."

They stare at me. I know exactly what they're thinking.

Noah says it anyway. "That's some righteous karma. Impaled on a fence post? Jesus."

"Let's get back to your story, even if Noah's right about the karma. Were you as smitten by Alan as everyone else?"

I shrug again. "Of course. Young and romantic, remember. Youthful stupidity is the worst kind. I never bothered much to flutter around Alan. There were so many others already doing so that I didn't think he'd even notice me, and then I got a boyfriend and didn't care anymore anyway." I grimace. "Then my boyfriend dumped me. I didn't take it well, and one day Alan found me in the woods, casting some not-nice spells at an effigy of my ex."

Jared makes a sad face, but Noah grins. "Really? That's epic. What kind of spells?"

"The standard ones. Stink and itch, of course, but also one that causes uncontrollable sweating. I was surprised when that worked on the effigy, but it was very satisfying, since I'd never cast spells like that on a living person."

"Of course not." Noah's gaze slides away. "That would be terrible. The sweating one would, at least. If that got out of control, a person could die of dehydration." There's a thoughtful note to his voice that confirms my impression of him being mean.

Jared mutters something about talking to Sam, and I figure it's probably best if I continue.

"Anyway, Alan didn't try anything with me. He helped me beat up the effigy, and then we sat and talked for a while. Even if he'd made a move, I wouldn't have been receptive to it then, and he knew it. I was surprised that I actually liked him, without all the... lothario charm. Before, he'd been that... that dreamy guy everyone swooned over, right? But I'd never heard anyone talk about what he was like aside from that. He was easy to talk to, and we had some common interests. We became friends."

Jared pushes aside his plate and props his elbow on the table. "This isn't how I expected the story to go."

Chuckling, I agree, "Past me didn't either. Alan was a good friend, though. He was still serial dating, which I didn't care about at all, but after about fifteen years, when he was between lovers, he asked me why I wouldn't give him a chance." The memories of that night rise, as clear as if it was yesterday. It's funny, because it wasn't particularly romantic or special. "We'd been out drinking and dancing, and we were still hyped up, laughing... sweaty. You know how it is."

They both make agreeing sounds.

"Alan said he'd fallen in love with me months ago and was just waiting for me to give him a sign. I was—" I laugh. "I was shocked. My mouth dropped open and I must have stuttered for a full minute. I didn't believe him—not that he loved me, but the type of love it was. We were friends, and I thought he was mixing his feelings up."

"I bet he loved being told that," Noah scoffs, and I shake my head.

"We argued about it, and then I told him I was happy for us to be friends who fucked, but he wasn't the commitment type, and I didn't expect him to change on my behalf." I pause reflectively. "I loved him as a friend, but not more, so I didn't think it would be a problem."

"A lot of this sounds familiar," Jared muses. "Dáithí, have you considered *not* offering to fuck your friends?"

I'm laughing even before Noah sprays soda all over his plate. "Eoin and I weren't truly friends, just friendly," I defend as I pass Noah my napkin. "And the thing with him was always romantic...ish. It just wasn't meant to be long-term."

Pinching the bridge of his nose, Jared says, "Mmm. Let's revisit that later. Go back to what you were saying about Alan."

"There's not much more to say. He wasn't going to turn down regular, no-strings sex, so we started doing that, but about six months later, he brought up the whole being-in-love-with-me thing again. By then..." I stop and think about all the feelings that were drowning me at the time. "We were friends, and we loved each other, and he was... Well, he was Alan. I'd started to think we could have more. Six months was almost his longest stretch of monogamy, and he wasn't showing any signs of wanting that to change. He swore that things were different with me because he loved me. That he'd changed—*I'd* changed him."

Noah groans. "Uh-oh."

"Yeah. I believed him. We were together for nearly fifty years after that, though I found out at the end that he hadn't been faithful for about eighteen of those. I loved him, and I was planning forever. We had a house together, a pet, even. He was just as affectionate and loving as always—nothing had changed over the years. I've thought about this so many times, but there were no signs for me to see."

"Did he just walk out?" Noah asks, and I shake my head.

"No, he came home one day and said he was moving to another settlement—this was before all the settlements were combined under one shield. He said he'd tried, but being committed to one person wasn't for him, and he felt trapped and stifled. He said that any love he'd ever felt for me had faded into misery." I keep my tone flat. Even after so long, those words hurt.

"I'm so sorry, Dáithí." Jared lays a hand over one of mine. "You know none of that was your fault."

"Fault doesn't matter. He was miserable, and I was heartbroken. I was lucky, in a way—for people who live as long as we do, the relationship was quite short. Imagine how hurt I could have been if it had lasted longer. I could have given him whole centuries, or even more." Those were the platitudes that got me through the months and years directly after he left. They feel almost as empty now as they did then.

"You think that's what Eoin would do?" Noah asks. "Cheat behind your back, then blame you for him being unhappy?"

"Absolutely not." I put heavy emphasis on both words. "Maybe the stuff with Alan skews my perspective in some ways, but I know who Eoin is, and he's not like that."

Jared opens his mouth, but I hold up a hand. "*But*, he's never been in a relationship, ever, and I'm not foolish enough to assume I've got a magic dick that changed him. I don't want to spend another fifteen years—or more—thinking I'm in a happy relationship, only to have my heart shattered again. I don't want to force Eoin to be someone he isn't."

An odd little silence falls. I'm not sure what they're thinking, but I'm wishing I didn't have to go back to work and could order a giant cocktail to wash away all the bad feelings I've dredged up.

"Dáithí," Jared says abruptly, "I just realized something."
"Oh?"
"This test we're setting up for Eoin... what if he passes?"
I freeze. "What?"

"What happens if Eoin passes whatever test you end up giving him?"

"Oooh," Noah hums. "Interesting."

My gaze flickers between them, and then around the room. "I-I... I don't know. I... *can* he pass?"

"That would be up to you and whatever test you decide on," Jared points out. "But if you set a standard and he meets it, whatever that is, would you accept it as proof of his commitment?"

"I-I-I..."

Noah cuts into my babbling, "What Jared's asking, Dáithí, is if you want Eoin to pass or fail? Because if you want him out of your life, we can come up with a test that's completely impossible to pass. But if you want him to have a chance at passing, well..." He shrugs. "I'm not saying we should make it easy for him, but if he *can* prove he's ready to commit, there are ways for him to do that."

My head spins. I'd never stopped to think about this. To consider that maybe Eoin could actually pass this test. The whole test thing was his idea, and I... didn't think it through.

"Is that an opportunity you want him to have?" Jared presses. "Dáithí, do you love Eoin, or think you could one day?"

I drag my gaze away from the wall and meet his. Do I love Eoin?

"Yes."

CHAPTER SEVEN

Eoin

IT'S NOT until Ari and Niamh stop talking about *I'm a Celebrity, Get Me Out of Here*—a show which, to the best of my understanding, rarely features an actual celebrity—that I start to pay attention. In fact, my whole team is oddly silent.

I look up.

Four frighteningly manic grins beam back at me. It's so disconcerting that it takes me a second to recognize them, and then I wonder what they're doing here. Caolan and Hagen might have a valid reason, but Alistair Smythe and Andrew Turner work for CSG, and I can't remember if either of them has even been in my office before.

Definitely none of them have a reason for pointing those horrible smiles at me.

"Are you lost?"

"Dude! Finally. Hagen said we couldn't interrupt because you get cranky when people interrupt you." Alistair bounds forward like an overgrown puppy—hellhound, I remind myself—and plants his ass on the edge of my desk. What is it with uninvited distractions sitting on my desk?

"There's a chair right there," I say, pointing, only to have Andrew slide into it.

"Thank you. This may take some time. We should all be comfortable."

That worries me more than the creepy smiles did. I glance around at my team, in case this is some sort of prank they've cooked up, but they all seem to be as confused as I am.

Which just leaves…

I narrow my eyes at Hagen. "You've known me long enough to know it's not just interruptions that make me cranky."

He holds up his hands, palms out. "I haven't done anything! I swear. Not yet, anyway."

My patience is wearing thin. Very, very thin. "Then maybe someone could tell me why you're all here?"

"It's like this," Alistair begins excitedly, way too much in my personal space. I roll my chair backward a little. "Noah came back from lunch and said he had a job for Team Bro, and dude, you have no idea how big of a miracle that is. Noah *hates* Team Bro. He's like, the anti-Bro. Which is sad, because Bros are epic, and Noah's epic too, just in a different way."

"It's true," Andrew murmurs.

"It's okay, though," Caolan assures me earnestly. "Noah might not want to be part of Team Bro—"

"Or want it to exist," Andrew interjects, smirking.

"—but he believes in utilizing resources properly, and he knows what our strengths are. We could totally do this."

"But then Hagen pointed out that you're *his* bro from way back, and of course that claim of bro-hood takes precedence. We won't do it without your okay," Alistair assures me.

They all look at me expectantly.

What the fuck?

"Listen, I don't know what you're talking about, but I'm

not having a great day—or week, to be honest—and there's some stuff going on in my personal life that—"

"Yeah, we know," Hagen interrupts. "Your situationship. That's why we're here."

I'm highly enough placed in the DEA to (maybe) get away with killing Hagen and Caolan, but it would cause an inter-government incident if I killed Alistair and Andrew... unless I made it look like an accident? Or... Alistair annoys a lot of people. Maybe the people at CSG would be so relieved, they'd let it slide?

Before I can decide whether my letter-opener or paper-weight would make a better weapon, Ari steps in. Literally steps in, taking Alistair's arm and pulling him off my desk, then standing between the two of us like a hellhound-saving barrier.

"Let's start again," he suggests. "Hagen, you explain. As much detail in as few sentences as possible." He raises his brows meaningfully. Hagen shoots a glance my way, then nods.

"Noah Cage had lunch today with Dáithí and Consort Jared," he begins, immediately getting my full attention. Dáithí has lunch with Jared fairly regularly, but I didn't think he knew Noah Cage more than to say hello in passing. Plus, he never mentioned having lunch plans. Sure, we were distracted last night, but—

"Dáithí told them you'd challenged him to set you a task that would prove your commitment to him and turn your situationship into a relationship," Hagen continues, and my lunch threatens to make a reappearance. He what?

"You *what*?" Ari exclaims. "Seriously?"

"Wait, Dáithí called it a situationship?" Brayan asks.

Hagen shakes his head. "No, that's me paraphrasing."

"Can we go back to the part where Eoin told Dáithí to *test him?*" Ari demands. "I don't think we're giving that enough attention."

"Can we go back to the reason you're all in my office?" As if it's not bad enough that everyone knows Dáithí doesn't want to be my boyfriend, now they're all going to know *why*.

"That's what I'm trying to tell you!" Hagen throws up his hands in exasperation while Caolan pats his back reassuringly. Alistair tsks.

I eye my letter-opener.

"Anyway, Dáithí asked for help to come up with the task, and Noah figured Team Bro would be perfect for the job. But like Al said, you and I have been bros since way before Noah was even born, so we won't do it unless you say it's okay." My ex-roommate and longtime friend looks at me expectantly. "It's your call, Eoin."

I rub my forehead and try not to let the despair and humiliation I'm feeling show. "Dáithí asked Noah for help testing me?"

Hagen nods. "Yeah."

"And Noah asked you all to help?"

This time, they all nod.

"Great. Just... great." I can't think of anything else to say. I was so hopeful last night that this might actually be a *chance* for me. A last-ditch one, sure, and okay, I had to twist Dáithí's arm to get him to agree, but it was better than him flat-out dumping me. This would give me an opportunity to convince him of my sincerity... not to mention give me more time with him, even if I failed.

Not that I planned to fail. I've been a soldier in the King's Army for a long time, and we don't consider failure to be an option. I *know* I can happily commit to a successful long-term relationship with Dáithí. I love him, and I don't want anything more than to spend my life with him. Passing any test designed to show that is completely possible.

Or at least, I thought it was. But I'm familiar with Hagen and his bros, with their wild plans and shenanigans. I've witnessed a lot of them and heard about more. If Dáithí wants them to help him plan this...

"He's setting me up to fail."

"Huh?"

I blink, then realize I said at least part of my inner monologue of despair out loud. Wonderful. Just a little more humiliation to add to the pile.

Everyone—including my team, who are somehow supposed to respect my leadership after this—is watching me, so I throw away the last few shreds of my pride and explain, "If Dáithí wants your help, he's not serious about giving me this chance to prove myself. He's humoring me—setting me up to fail so he can just end things like he wanted to and go on with his life."

"Actually," Andrew begins, but Ari interrupts.

"Dáithí wanted to end things? You challenged him to test you? What is going on, Eoin? When did all this happen? Does the king know?"

I'm starting to think my colleagues might be too involved in my personal life. "Why would the king know?" I ask incredulously. "I'm not going to let it affect my work."

"As exemplary as that is, it doesn't answer Ari's other questions," a very familiar voice says, and if I didn't already know how disastrous it can be to mess with time, I'd be trying to create a spell to erase the last ten minutes of my life.

"Hello, Your Majesty," Alistair greets cheerfully. "You're looking good. How's your honey doing? I've been meaning to call him."

My hand actually twitches with the need to reach for my letter-opener. Alistair's big, and he's well-trained, but I'm a strong fighter myself, and I'll have the advantage of surprise.

"Jared's very well, thank you. He mentioned the other day

that he hasn't spoken to you for a while, so I'm sure he'd appreciate that call." King Raðulfr is, as always, gracious, even when speaking to an insouciant hellhound. I square my shoulders and look toward the doorway, only to see that the situation is worse than I thought.

The king brought Brandt with him. Because clearly this mess needed another dragon.

"Your Majesty," I interrupt. "We were just…" There's no intelligent way to finish that sentence. "Was there something you needed?"

"We're here for you," Brandt declares gleefully, striking horror all the way to my bones.

"What Brandt means," the king corrects, "is that Jared called to tell me what happened at lunch, and we thought we'd come and offer our support. If there's anything you need from us while you're proving yourself to Dáithí, you have only to ask. Do you need some time off?"

"No! I mean… no, thank you, Your Majesty." How did this get so far out of my control? "You're very kind, but this is basically the death knell for my hopes. Dáithí has asked Team Bro to develop the test. It's clear he doesn't want me to pass."

Andrew leans forward. "Actually—"

"It's not like Dáithí to be mean-spirited like that," Brandt says, frowning. "Petty, yes—we all love how petty he can be. Nobody devises harmless revenge like Dáithí."

A murmur of agreement runs through the room. We've *all* been on the receiving end of Dáithí's petty vengeance at some stage or other, since none of us are smart enough to keep from pissing him off.

The king purses his lips. "Did you say before that he wanted to break up?"

I nod. "Yes. Last night, he said he knew I wanted more from him and he felt it would be better to end things between us."

"Ohhhh." The chorus of disappointed groans is balm for my bruised feelings.

"That's when I... well, I guess I panicked, though it didn't feel like it at the time. We argued about it for a while, and when he said he didn't want a relationship with me because I'm not commitment material"—that still stings—"I challenged him to test me. I said he could devise any task he wanted, over any timeframe he wanted, and I'd prove that I was committed to him... us." I wince. "I thought it would give me a chance to change his mind."

"Ballsy," Alistair says admiringly. "Tell me, are you happy with your current bros?"

"Recruit later," Hagen tells him. "This doesn't make sense. You think Dáithí wants us to help so we'll, what, create a test that's impossible to pass?"

I shrug. "Doesn't he? Why else would he ask you?"

"Actu—"

"Noah asked us," Caolan points out. "Maybe Dáithí doesn't even know?"

"Nah." Alistair shakes his head. "Noah wouldn't have brought us in without checking it was okay."

"Hagen's right," Ari points out. "You told Dáithí the test could take as long as he wanted, right? That's what you meant by 'any timeframe'?"

"Yeah." I frown as I realize what he's getting at.

"So why would he need them if he wanted something you could never pass? All he'd need to do is set up something—anything—with a long timeframe. Decades or even centuries. It could be super simple, and if he really believes you're not commitment material, then he'd expect you to give up on it sooner or later anyway."

Huh. That's true. But... "Dáithí's too soft-hearted to do something like that. He tried to break up because he knew I was so invested. He'd never string me along if he could give me a clean break." I sink back into the gloom of knowing Dáithí doesn't even want to try.

The sound of a throat being cleared brings my head back up. Andrew gives me a wry smile. "If I could have your attention for a moment, I may be able to shed some light on this."

Alistair frowns. "What—"

"Alistair, I swear, if I get interrupted *one more time*, I will rip your throat out and laugh from the joy of it." He holds up one hand, letting his claws out. Vampires are deceptively creepy.

Alistair closes his mouth.

"Thank you. Now, as I was saying, Noah and Jared asked Dáithí if this should be a test you can pass... and he said yes."

I blink, then blink again. My ears start to ring. "He said... yes?"

Andrew nods. "I specifically asked Noah about this while Alistair was calling the others. The test is to be a fair one, a genuine chance for you to prove yourself... or not."

The grin that splits my face is so wide, my cheeks hurt. Around the office, there are cheers and back-slapping.

"Well," Raðulfr says, smiling. "That's more like it."

"So, what's the word?" Hagen asks. "Are we helping, or not?"

I don't know how wild of a test "Team Bro" will come up with, but it's hard to care. Dáithí wants me to have a chance at succeeding. Who cares what the test is? "Yes."

CHAPTER EIGHT

Dáithí

WHEN I ASKED Jared and Noah for help, I had no idea what I was getting into. Even though I agreed to their suggestion of finding "experts," I didn't think I'd end up in the boardroom after hours with a hellhound waving a whiteboard marker at me.

Meh. There are worse things.

I do a quick tally of who's here: Jared, looking surprisingly smug, Noah and his husband, Andrew, Caolan, Hagen—I give him a narrow-eyed warning glare. I've had to deal with his chaos before—and Alistair, who I also glare at. Everyone in the building knows Alistair. He throws a great party, but for those of us trying to run an office, he's trouble.

Noah was right about bringing these guys in on this. Team Bro, as they call themselves, has the perfect skill set for a job like this. Let's just hope they understand the objective.

Nervous hope flutters in my chest, and I ruthlessly shred it. There will be no hoping. Maybe—possibly—there's a tiny chance that Eoin will pass whatever test Team Bro devises. It's far more likely that I'm right and he'll lose interest or decide he's ready to move on instead. Letting myself hope now is only going to make it hurt more when that happens, and the whole point of this is to prevent that hurt.

Alistair finishes writing "The True Love Challenge" on the whiteboard and puts the marker down so he can clap his hands. "Settle down! We have a lot to get through tonight."

"We've been waiting for you," Noah points out.

Ignoring him, Alistair continues, "On behalf of Team Bro, I'd like to thank Dáithí for including us in this endeavor. We appreciate the trust you're placing in us for this vitally important task." He smiles at me.

"Uh... yes. You come highly recommended. And I've seen examples of your work." That must be the right thing to say, because all four "bros" sit up straighter. "I want to be clear, though, that no glitter will be involved." I love me some sparkle just as much as the next guy, but I can't think of any situation when glitter will be needed to test Eoin's capacity for commitment. Plus, that shit is impossible to clean up, and the last thing I need when this is over and I'm recovering from a bruised heart is to be finding glitter everywhere.

Alistair sighs, and Hagen shakes his head. "Of course there won't be any glitter," he says. "We know how to assess when it's event-appropriate."

"Do you, though?" Noah asks, and thinking back on the number of times they've brought glitter to the CSG and DEA offices, I have to agree with him.

Hagen opens his mouth, but closes it again when Caolan elbows him and says, "We're wasting time. This discussion isn't an efficient use of our resources. Al, bro, sorry, but I'm canceling the rest of your speech and moving to the next item on the agenda."

Jared leans toward me and murmurs, "Do you have a copy of the agenda? I didn't get one."

I can only shake my head, too shocked by the knowledge that there's an agenda—that's apparently broken down by time increments—to speak.

"I understand," Alistair says, joining us at the table and taking a seat.

"Am I dreaming?" Noah asks. "What is happening here?"

Andrew kisses his cheek and pats his arm. "Caolan is Team Bro's coordinator. He learned a lot from David about task management and planning. How else do you think we manage to pull off such perfectly executed activities?"

The temptation to laugh is so strong that I bite my lip. I know David Carew, Caolan's boyfriend, well enough to know he'd be horrified if he found out he'd inadvertently helped with Team Bro's shenanigans.

"Please turn your attention to the screen," Caolan orders, and the wall monitor beside the whiteboard comes to life. "We didn't have a great deal of time for preparation, but we've pulled together some basic background. Tonight's decisions will shape the direction of further research."

"This is incredible." Jared sounds impressed. "It's only been a few hours."

"This is overkill," I counter, staring at the split screen showing photos and short bios of me and Eoin. "You don't need—" The screen changes to a dot-pointed list headed by the title "The Situationship." It's a summary of what's happened since Eoin and I started dating.

"That's such a stupid word," Noah declares. "Situationship? Really?"

"Meh." I consider. "It kind of fits. But none of this is necessary."

"Of course it is," Caolan insists. "How can we devise a plan without any background?"

Maybe he's right. I've spent the past year flying by the

seat of my pants, hoping that Eoin would stay interested and yet not letting myself get too invested in preparation for the day his interest wanes. My big plan this week, when I realized that strategy wasn't working anymore, was to end things before either of us could get seriously hurt.

Clearly, that didn't happen.

Instead, I agreed to give him the chance to prove himself, and somehow ended up here, with Team Bro giving a very professional-looking presentation. Maybe their plan is going to be better than my lack of one.

"Okay." I sit back. "We'll do it your way."

"You were going to anyway," Alistair tells me. "But I'm glad we didn't have to convince you. The first question we have is about the scope of the challenge. Does it need to be a single task?"

Jared's breath catches, and he props his elbow on the table, chin in palm. "Interesting. Multiple criteria would be more effective for assessing the outcome."

I slowly turn to look at him. "Is that a teacher thing? Are you being a kindergarten teacher right now?"

He shrugs. "It's not exclusive to teaching. The best way to assess something is to look at several key elements, not just one."

"Exactly," Hagen says. "Dáithí, c'mon, you've seen me do this before. When we're building a bridge, we don't pick the spot based only on the proximity to the town. We look at a whole bunch of stuff first. The only true way to determine Eoin wants a committed relationship is for him to be in one until he dies. That's the ultimate proof. Since that's not something you're willing to try without assurances, we need to look at other measures."

Guilt and self-loathing swamp me. "This is wrong. Eoin doesn't deserve—"

"No." Andrew holds up his hand to stop me. "This was

Eoin's idea, remember? He told you to test him. Unless you've changed your mind and are ready to make your relationship official, the best way to show your respect for him is to let him try to win you over."

I'm still a little nauseated by the thought, but he's right. I want—desperately want, have always wanted—to throw caution to the wind and dive headlong into being Eoin's boyfriend, but I truly don't think it's what he wants, and I'm not putting myself through that again. When he realizes, partway through these tests, that we're not meant to be, he'll be grateful to me. We can continue on as friends, probably, and yes, I'll be a little bruised by the loss of him, but nowhere near what I would be if I let myself love him.

He'd be so easy to love.

I swallow hard. "How many did you have in mind?"

The bros grin at me in a way that makes me think of glitter bombs and hidden plastic ducks. I may have unleashed a monster... or a team of them.

"I'm so glad you asked." Caolan gestures with a flourish to the screen, and I see that it's changed to another bulleted list, this one titled "Objectives." They really have given this some thought. I can't believe they put it all together in a few hours. "As you can see," he continues, "we've broken this down into subsections. The overall goal is for Eoin to prove he's 'relationship material,'"—Caolan actually makes air quotes with his fingers—"but that can mean a lot of things, and we also want to show that he's relationship material *for you*, specifically."

I hadn't considered that. It's not a bad point. The last thing I want is to prove Eoin would make a great boyfriend for someone else.

"It's not up for debate that Eoin is capable of maintaining commitments," Hagen says, taking over. "Dáithí, I'm sure you agree with that."

"Yes, of course." I nod. "He's committed to the king and to his service to the DEA—before that, the King's Army. He's loyal to his friends. You're a good example of that, since anyone with less loyalty would have ghosted you millennia ago."

He folds his arms across his chest. "Rude. I'm an excellent friend."

I wave that off. "Whatever. The point is, I agree that Eoin is capable of commitment—it's not something lacking in him. But there's a big difference between a job and friends and your life partner."

"And that's why we're here. To start with, we're going to test his dedication to commitment—"

"But you just said—"

"—when there's no element of expectation," Hagen finishes. "With a job, there's a requirement to deliver. There's a boss and colleagues, and if you stop performing or showing up, there are consequences. The same with friends—if you never join in or answer calls, there's someone who can call you out for it."

"What the fuck are you talking about?" Noah demands.

"We're saying that to truly test Eoin's ability to commit, we need to do so without him knowing," Alistair announces mysteriously.

Noah looks at him like he just said the sun was green. Jared and I exchange glances, and he shrugs.

"I'm guessing you have ideas for that, so let's move on. What else are you planning to test?"

"How he relates to you," Andrew replies. "How well he knows you and how he behaves in reaction to things you do and say—or situations you're in."

Jared perks up. "Oooh. That could be fun."

"None of this is fun," I remind him. "Why doesn't this meeting have chocolate?" Or booze.

"It's going to be fun," Alistair assures me. "At least, it will be if Eoin lives up to my expectations." He holds up his arm, and for the first time, I see the pink wristband on it. "I'm on Team Success."

"Team... Success?" The words are spelled out in black letters against the pink.

"How did you have time to have those made?" Noah demands. "Did you get *any* work done this afternoon? You're already behind on your reports."

"Who's on Team Failure?" I ask. It's a logical question, but Caolan gasps.

"Not any of us," he assures me, holding out his wrist for me to see. "We're all on Team Success." His lip curls. "We did have some of the other bands made, though. In case anyone has poor judgment."

"They're vomit green," Hagen adds helpfully.

"I'll have one of each."

The shocked silence that takes over the room is kind of nice.

"Dáithí," Jared begins, but I shake my head.

"I'm neutral. I have to be, if I'm going to get through this." That's what I'll keep repeating to myself, anyway. "I don't mind if you all pick sides, as long as you don't let your work be biased."

"Never!" Alistair shakes his head vehemently. "I am fully confident that Eoin will prove himself without any assistance from us. He will succeed!"

Okay, he might be losing sight of the point. "You know it's okay if he doesn't, right? That will just mean that he's changed his mind about what he wants. There's no win or lose here." I'm going to keep telling myself *that*, as well.

"So it's okay with you if Eoin has a support team?" Hagen challenges.

"What do you mean?"

"We're here to help you plan the tests. Is it okay with you if Eoin has people to help him carry them out?"

I think about it. "Theoretically, yes. But doesn't that defeat the purpose of what we're doing, if someone else is completing the tasks for him?"

"I'd say that depends on the tasks."

CHAPTER NINE

Eoin

HOW LONG CAN this damn meeting last? I'm still not clear on why there had to be a meeting to begin with. How hard can it be to come up with a test of some kind? I lived with Hagen for decades, so I know exactly how weirdly creative he is. Something like this should be easy for him. All he and his Team Bro friends had to do was give Dáithí a couple of suggestions to choose from. It could have been an email.

So why am I still sitting here at Raðulfr's condo an hour after the meeting was supposed to start, sweating through my shirt and resisting the urge to get very drunk on my boss's whiskey?

"Maybe Dáithí changed his mind," I blurt—not for the first time. "What if he decided he doesn't want to do this after all?"

Ari nudges my glass closer. "Have a sip to calm your nerves."

I shake my head. "No, I—"

"That wasn't a suggestion. Have a damn sip before I choke you."

"What Ari means," Raðulfr interjects, "is that the whiskey will take the edge off your nerves while we wait. Someone would have called or texted if Dáithí had changed his mind."

Would they? "What if they haven't because they're trying to talk him back into it?"

The sound that emerges from Ari's throat convinces me to pick up my glass and have a tiny sip. He's the most level-headed, easygoing person on my team. If he's this annoyed with me, I'm probably overreacting to the situation.

Though I'm not sure it's possible to overreact to the possibility of losing the love of your life.

I chug until my glass is empty.

"Impressive," Brandt says. "Refill?" He's pouring before I can answer.

A responsible team leader probably wouldn't act this way in front of half his team, his boss who is the co-head of government, and the other co-head of government. Too bad I'm not wearing my "responsible" hat right now. I knock the second glass back as fast as the first.

It's outside work hours anyway, and I long ago mastered spells for sobering up. It might do my team good to know I'm a *person* with *feelings*.

Wow, the effects of that whiskey hit *fast*.

"What are you all here for?" I ask in a desperate attempt to distract myself from the wait and everyone else from my out-of-character behavior. I look around the table at my team. "Go home. Except for whoever's on duty." Fuck. Who's on duty tonight?

I tip my head back and squint at the ceiling, which seems to be rotating. "That's an interesting design feature."

"What is?" Brayan asks, but I'm too busy following the movement of the ceiling with my eyes to answer. It's slowly spinning, but not in a perfect circle—there are all kinds of wavy dips and—

"Whoa!" Hands grab me and lift me back into my chair.

"I thought that was only his first drink?" Niamh says, hovering beside me as Ari grabs my chin and turns my face toward him, peering into my eyes.

I grin at him. "Hi. You have a nice face."

"Hm," Raðulfr says as Ari's jaw drops. I pat his cheek. "Where did you say you got this whiskey, Brandt?"

Brandt's already examining the bottle. "Fabian got it for me. I didn't have time to stop somewhere, and it's not like I can ask *my* security team to go to the liquor store for me."

Oh! I swivel in my chair and nearly fall off again—it's okay, Ari catches me. Who knew he was so good at that?— and wave excitedly at Steffen, who's sitting at the far end of the long table, a little apart from the rest of us. Hey, this table really is long!

"How many people does this table seat?" I ask, then wave at Steffen again. "Do you have time for a consult? Raðulfr's been troublesome lately."

The king's low laugh always makes me happy. It's not easy being the person who sometimes has to say "no" to my species leader. "I just want you to be safe and happy," I tell him earnestly.

Steffen's chair scrapes across the floorboards as he stands abruptly. "Where are you going?" Brandt asks him.

"To call Wil. He needs to check if Fabian has any more of that whiskey and confiscate it."

"Sit down. Fabian's allowed to drink whiskey." Brandt leans back in his chair, utterly relaxed, but Steffen's not having it. He points at me.

"Do you see that? Do you see what *two* glasses of that concoction did to a steady, reliable, *responsible* man? Imagine what it could do to Fabian—or Dustin—or *Hagen?*" His expression turns even sterner than usual. "I'm drafting an edict for you to sign. That whiskey is going to be banned for all dragons."

Brandt purses his lips, studying me, then sighs. "I suppose that's the sensible thing to do."

I gasp. Steffen's stern face worked! Would it work on Raðulfr too? I should practice, just in case I need it one day.

"What's wrong with his face?" Brayan cries. "Is he having a medical emergency?"

Fingers press against my neck, and I feel the cool tingle of a spell wash over me—Ari's. He's got the most training with healing magic, which makes him the team medic. "You have skills to go with your nice face," I inform him, even as said nice face relaxes.

"He's fine, just drunk. Why were you making that weird expression?" He sits back down in his chair, still turned toward me.

"I was practicing Steffen's stern face. Oh! Steffen, is it okay if I use your stern face?" Has the word "face" been used too much tonight?

The frown line between Steffen's eyebrows lightens a little, which is practically a smile for him, and I take that as permission.

"Seriously," Niamh says, "what's in this?" She's picked up the whiskey bottle and is studying the label. "And why has it only affected Eoin like this? We all had some."

"Don't worry about it," I tell her. "A little drunk never hurt me. I've been waaaaaay drunker than this."

"Have you?" Raðulfr asks, sounding amused. I did that! I amused my king.

"I'm so sorry I don't get to make you happy more," I tell him solemnly. "You deserve to be happy. Jared is a gift in your life."

"He is," he agrees. "Don't worry, Eoin. I know you're

doing your best to protect me. It's okay if that means you can't make me happy all the time."

"Yes!" I jab a finger toward him, then turn to Ari. "See? See how right he is. Sometimes we have to make him miserable so he can be safe for Jared to make him happy! Jared is his happiness."

Ari grabs my finger, which for some reason is still pointing at... something, and pulls my arm down to rest on the table. "Uh-huh."

"Dáithí is my happiness." Ohhh. Dáithí. "But he might not want to be. It's hard work, being someone's happiness, even though all Dáithí has to do is exist. He's... he's my sunshine." I squint, because that's not right. Sunshine is mellow, not sassy. "The kind that sometimes gives you a little sunburn, but you love it and want to spend all your time out in it anyway."

"Maybe don't tell him that," Niamh suggests, and I swing around to frown at her. She's swaying, for some reason.

"Why? Do you think he doesn't want to be my sunshine? You do, don't you? You think he's changed his mind about giving me a chance."

"I meant the sunburn part," she says patiently. "Calling him a sunburn isn't romantic. Or a compliment."

"It's a *metaphor*," I explain. "Dáithí's all hot and burny and sometimes has flaming explosions on the outside, but inside, he's sweet and funny and perfect. Like the sun."

"Don't tell him that either," Brayan advises. "Also, I'm not an expert on the sun, but I don't think it's 'sweet and funny' on the inside. I was told it's a ball of gas."

Are they deliberately missing the point? "Even a ball of gas can be sweet and funny."

Niamh opens her mouth, but the king speaks before she can. "Let's not worry about that for now. We all know what you meant, Eoin, and I think it's wonderful that you see Dáithí like that."

"It's not how I see him; it's how he is." Why are there suddenly two of him? Is this an illusion spell—maybe a new security measure? I should know about that, since I'm the head of his security team. Leaning toward Ari—who puts a hand on my shoulder and pushes me back into my chair—I whisper, "Did I authorize the two-Raðulfrs illusion spell?"

He glances across the table at the king, then back at me. "You're seeing two of him?"

I nod. For some reason, my head keeps moving up and down even after I want it to stop, so I grab my chin with my hand. "Two."

"Uh-huh. You did approve it. We're, uh, testing it tonight, remember."

"Of course I remember. I was just checking that you did. Good job." I'm so glad he's my second-in-command.

"I think I've worked it out," Brandt says suddenly. He's holding the whiskey bottle in one hand and his phone in the other, staring intently at the screen. "This is a community brand, which means sorcery to prevent them from metabolizing the alcohol too fast. Their website says the weave they use is their own patented design, since they only produce whiskey, which is supposed to be sipped." He looks over at me. "Eoin definitely did not sip."

"So the effects of the weave are amplified because he drank it fast?" Steffen asks suspiciously. He's adorable sometimes.

"Steffen, you're adoramph—" Ari's hand clamping over my mouth cuts me off.

Steffen frowns. "What did he say?"

"Nothing that would add value to this conversation—or his life." Ari smiles at Steffen, then leans closer to me and murmurs, "I'm going to take my hand away. Do not speak."

I nod, my eyes darting around the room. Is there danger? Have I been compromised? Will my voice trigger a detonation spell? I won't risk Raðulfr, but Ari seems to have things under control, so for now I'll let him take the lead.

"I guess so," Brandt is saying. "Alcohol does affect us, after all. It just wears off faster, making it difficult for enough to build up in the bloodstream to make us tipsy or drunk. Before the community began using sorcery to help with that, the trick to feeling a buzz was to drink a lot in a short space of time. Eoin did that, but since he wasn't drinking human liquor..."

Raðulfr raises a brow. "Should we worry about how you know this?"

"You used to come to Earth back then too," Brandt teases. "Don't try to tell me you didn't chug that fermented grain and fruit mixture I have such fond memories of." The king merely smiles, and Brandt continues, "Anyway, what Eoin did was the equivalent of having half a dozen strong drinks in two minutes."

That's fascinating. "I love science!"

"I don't think it's science, exactly," Ari says. "Should we sober him up?"

My king studies me, and I smile widely at him. "Not yet. Let's wait for an update first."

This sounds like something I should know about. "What kind of update? Do I need to be briefed?"

"Will he remember this later?" Niamh asks. "If not, we missed a big opportunity by not recording any of it."

"Will who remember what?" I demand. "I think I need to be briefed on whatever's going on." I'm in charge of Raðulfr's security, after all. It concerns me that I've been left out of the loop on— "Ooooh! These chairs vibrate!"

"They do?" Brandt twists around to look at his chair.

"Mine doesn't—did I get a dud? Raðulfr, how dare you give me a dud chair! I insist on swapping for a vibrating one."

Ari sighs. "It's probably your phone. Why don't you take it out of your pocket?"

My jaw drops open. "I bet you're right! You're so smart. I'm lucky to have a friend like you." I grope at the side of my pants. "I can't find my pocket! Can you find it and get my phone for me?"

"No," he replies, grabbing my hand and moving it higher up my leg. "We're not that kind of friends. Try here."

I'm still puzzling over what he could mean by that when my fingertips brush against hard metal. My phone!

Unfortunately, even when I finally get it out of my suddenly too-small pocket and see a message notification from Hagen, I can't access the message. My stupid phone keeps rejecting my code. "Third time lucky," I mutter, but before I can punch in the digits, Ari snatches it from my hand.

"What's the code?"

I gape at him. All these years working together, and he wants me to share a personal security code? He should know better. "Sharing unlock codes is a breach of security protocol," I remind him.

"Yeah, but if you input the wrong code again, you'll be locked out, and since I just watched you hit the same number six times in a row, I'm pretty sure you can't see the keypad clearly right now. Code?"

"Of course I can see—"

"Code?" he insists, sounding like he did before when he threatened to choke me. Sighing, I give in and tell him. It's not going to work for him, either, so when I eventually get in I can just change—

"Okay, that worked."

What? "Impossible!" How did it work for him when it didn't for me?

"Hagen says they'd like to join us and present the tasks. I'm telling him yes, right?"

There's a chorus of agreement from around the table, and I belatedly say, "Yes." Then I add, "Who's coming here why?"

Raðulfr sighs. "Time to sober him up."

Sober who up?

The cool touch of Ari's magic is the next thing I know.

CHAPTER TEN

Dáithí

THIS WHOLE DAY has been so weird, and I guess it's about to get weirder, because I'm standing in front of the king's door, waiting for Jared to unlock it. Apparently, when I called in Team Bro, I started a chain reaction, and now both of the heads of my government are waiting inside, along with Eoin and some of his teammates, who are here to support him.

I mean, I can see why it's fair for him to have support, but does it have to include our bosses?

The door opens at last, and I follow Jared through it, Noah right behind me and Team Bro boisterously bringing up the rear. They're way more excited about all of this than I am.

King Raðulfr is walking toward us, the little smile on his face that he always gets when Jared's around, and just like always, a longing-jealousy combo moment hits me. I hate that I have this reaction to seeing how happy and in love they are, because I really am thrilled for them. The king's been alone for a long time, and all of us who've worked with him have wanted him to find love again. Jared is perfect for him, and I *like* Jared. I genuinely consider him a friend, and I don't want to be that person who's jealous of his friend's happiness.

But seeing them fit so perfectly together turns me into a green-eyed... whatever it is that jealous people are. I want Eoin to look at me that way, as if a few hours apart felt like centuries, as if seeing me is the best part of his day. And I want it to last forever.

I swallow hard as that stubborn tendril of hope tries to rise again. Searching for a distraction, I look around, taking in the details of the condo. The doors opened into a huge living-dining room. The furniture is all nice, but it seems a little sterile. I wonder if there's another living area somewhere, because I can't see either the king's or Jared's personality here.

That dining table is fucking huge, though. Line another one the same size up beside it and stick some mattresses on top, and you could host one heck of an orgy.

My gaze catches on Eoin, standing beside the table. His face is pale and drawn. I'm crossing the room before I realize it.

"What's wrong? Are you sick?" He was fine when he left the office for the day—a little subdued, maybe, since he knew I was planning to test him, but not like this. He looks awful.

He shakes his head. "No, just tired. The healing spell—"

"*Healing?*" My voice rises, but I barely notice the room falling quiet. I'm too busy unbuttoning Eoin's shirt, looking for where he might have been wounded. "What happened? Where are you—"

His hands close over mine as I reach for his belt. "Dáithí. I'm fine."

"But—"

"Look at me."

I raise my gaze to his, and the steadiness there eases my panic. Whatever happened, he's okay. "Why did you need to be healed?"

He grimaces. "Ari got me drunk."

My "What?" is echoed more explosively by Ari.

"I did not," he adds. "I told you to take a sip, not down the whole glass in one swallow."

Ugh. Drinking games? Really? And in the king's home? I guess they'll never grow out of that behavior. Irritation burns away the last of my concern, and I step back, freeing my hands from Eoin's grasp. He frowns a little, but immediately sets to work on the buttons I undid, and heat rises to my cheeks as I realize how many people witnessed my... momentary break in composure.

Definitely not a panicked meltdown.

"Wait, he was drunk, and it got healed?" Alistair asks. "Like... completely healed, no more drunk, no hangover?" He turns to Caolan. "Bro, have you been holding out on me? How come you never mentioned this? You've seen me suffering through hangovers!"

Caolan shrugs. "Healing magic isn't my area. I only know spells for basic wound care, and only because it was part of my training when I joined the army."

"And the no-drunk spell wasn't part of that?" Alistair seems offended by that idea.

I glance at Noah, and we both roll our eyes. "Oddly enough, the King's Army didn't think soldiers would need to heal hangovers while they were on duty," I point out.

"Boy, were they wrong," Hagen mutters, and His Majesty's brows shoot up.

"This may be a conversation I'm not supposed to be part of," he suggests mildly, and I have the satisfaction of seeing Hagen wince.

"It's also off topic," Noah adds. "I want to get home at some point, so can we do what we came here for?" He settles himself into one of the chairs at the table and looks around expectantly.

I immediately sit in the chair closest to me, nerves

flooding in now that it seems like the time is actually here. We're going to give Eoin the list of tasks, and...

Well, either he'll accept them, or he won't.

People find places to sit, and soon the sound of scraping chair legs gives way to quiet. "So," the king says, "Dáithí, you have the floor."

That's not at all scary. "Team Bro pointed out that the only single task that could give an accurate answer to the question at hand would be for Eoin to be in a long-term committed relationship, which makes this a chicken and egg situation."

Beside me, Eoin stirs. "Hm. Can't prove I'm relationship material without being in one, and you don't want to be in one until I prove it."

I open my mouth to refute that—I *do* want it, I'm just not convinced he does—but since everyone here has no doubt heard all those details already, it's not worth repeating them. Instead, I say, "To combat this, Team Bro suggested a series of tasks that will assess elements that are contributing factors of a long-term commitment. Since they're all in long-term committed relationships themselves, it can be argued that they're subject-matter experts."

There's a tiny pause as those of us with a claim to sanity ponder the validity of that statement.

"More than one task?" Eoin asks, leaning back in his chair. "No problem."

Ari, who's sitting on his other side, sighs. "What he meant was, the original agreement was for a single test, not an open-ended series of them."

I nod approvingly, glad someone on Eoin's team—because there's no question Ari would be—is thinking clearly. "Yes, we—"

"That's not what I meant," Eoin argues. "If it's going to take more than one test for me to prove myself, that's fine by me. I'm here for one, one dozen, or one hundred tasks, if that's what it takes."

The twin feelings of guilt and yearning adoration battle within me, and my next words come unbidden. "You should hold yourself in higher esteem. Why aren't you demanding—"

"Before this gets out of hand," Noah interrupts, raising his voice to talk over me, "Andrew's going to explain the plan. Save your questions until the end, and don't have any questions."

"I already have a question," Niamh says, then raises her hands when Noah shoots her a look that should cause burns. "I changed my mind. No questions."

Noah aims that same expression around the table, and when everyone stays silent, he gestures to his husband. "Speak."

Smiling at him fondly, Andrew says, "But Caolan hasn't set up the presentation."

Caolan pushes back from the table. "Is there a television somewhere? It would only take a minute to—"

"We don't need the presentation," I snap, feeling a sudden kinship with Noah. Why is everyone determined to drag this out? "Sit down, Caolan. Andrew?" He's grinning now, which makes me suspect he did that deliberately.

"Yes, of course. As Dáithí said, we've put together a series of tasks, each of which is designed to highlight a strength—or lack thereof—that's needed in a happy relationship. While the nature of each task is such that only Eoin can complete it, we encourage him to assemble a support team to help with preparation. As Caolan pointed out, having separate friendship groups as well as a shared one can be an important part of a healthy relationship."

It's true, and good advice, but I'm still convinced his boyfriend only said it to him to keep from being sucked into Team Bro.

"Wait, what?" Eoin straightens, frowning. "I can do this on my own. I don't want any question of whether I only succeeded because I had help."

Ugh! "Why are you like this? You should be offended by this whole thing, not trying to make it even harder for yourself. You're so stubborn."

His jaw drops. "Me, stubborn? Have you looked in a mirror lately? The only reason we're doing this is because you can't accept that you're special enough to make *anyone* want to commit to you, even someone who never has before!"

"That is *not*—"

"Oh my god, shut up!" Noah yells.

The resulting silence is broken by Jared. "You two are so sweet, the way you try to defend each other from... each other."

I'm still glaring at Eoin, so I see the exact moment my dawning sheepishness is reflected on his face. He clears his throat. "Continue."

Andrew smirks. He's done that a lot tonight, and it's particularly annoying. "The existence of your support team isn't up for debate. Dáithí has us, so you also get people. While Dáithí will have the final overall say on whether you've proved yourself or not, since apparently it's not legal to force people to be in a relationship—"

"What?" Eoin says.

I wave off his question. "I'll explain later. Please don't ask." That was a whole conversation I never thought I'd have. At one point, I thought Noah was going to single-handedly rip out Alistair's spleen.

"Ahem. As I was saying, Dáithí will have the final word, but both teams will be involved in the assessment of each task and will give feedback. He'll take that feedback into consideration when he makes his decision."

Eoin's brows draw together, and I resist the urge to

wring my hands. There's a good chance he'll object now. "Wait, whether I pass each test is going to be decided by a panel?"

"Essentially, yes."

Ari's nodding. "That's good. Very fair."

"I don't know," Eoin says slowly, causing his friend to groan. "I don't want Dáithí to feel pressured into his decision."

How—*how*—has he managed to stay alive for so long with so few self-preservation instincts? I bite back the urge to yell, and instead take a deep breath. "I won't feel pressured," I assure him, and I'm proud of how calm I sound. "This is an important decision, and it wouldn't be fair to either of us if I let people railroad me."

He still seems unsure, so I add, "If I can resist the pressure from Jax at Smooth as Butter to accept a thirty percent discount on services in exchange for letting them put a temporary tattoo of their business logo on my ass, then I can resist whatever pressure this lot puts on me."

Eoin's concern melts into a laugh, probably remembering the first time I told him about that, and I wink. It's become an inside joke between us, him asking me every time I have an appointment if Jax is still offering the deal.

"What's Smooth as Butter?" Niamh asks.

"And why would they want to put their business logo on your... butt?" Jared adds, perplexed.

Grinning, Eoin replies, "It's where Dáithí goes for waxing."

Alistair's delighted shout almost drowns out my answer for Jared. "Advertising."

His mouth forms a shocked O, and then his cheeks flush bright red. "For waxing... Okay. I always wanted to ask someone who got waxed down there... it hurts, right?"

Oh, that sweet little thing. I'm tempted to tease, but the

fierce expression on His Majesty's face changes my mind. "Yes. A lot." I shrug. "I think it's worth it, though."

"Hmm." Eoin leans over to murmur in my ear, "I do too."

Now it's my turn to blush. I don't know why—I've never been the kind of person who's shy about sex or anatomy. There's something about Eoin's appreciative little growl, though, that makes me feel like a shy virgin... who wants to be debauched.

I clear my throat. "Is it time to talk about the tasks?"

CHAPTER ELEVEN

Eoin

THE SIGHT of Dáithí's sexy flush makes my whole day so much better. Of course, it started feeling less like a tragedy when he walked in the door, proving that he hadn't changed his mind, and then went all fierce protector on me, worrying that I might have been hurt.

He loves me. I know he does. He's just scared of being hurt. It breaks my heart that he doesn't know I'd rather die a thousand painful deaths than cause him a moment of grief, but I can understand how it might be hard for him to accept that someone with my track record suddenly wants forever. Words are easy in situations like this, which is why I'm hoping this challenge will back them up with actions. Ari might have been unhappy with the idea of more than one test, but I welcome the chance to show, over and over, that I'm not the same fuckboy—to use an Earth term—that I used to be.

I'm older. I've been through a lot, and watched the people close to me go through it too. I've lost so many friends, I can't count, even though their faces haunt me. I've seen my people establish new lives, safe at last to exist and love... and

I want that too. I want the security of this new home and a love I can rely on.

But the only person I want it with is Dáithí. I won't settle for anyone else. So I'll happily complete any test set to prove that and win my future.

"The tasks," Andrew Turner announces, then turns to Hagen, who's been quiet since his inadvertent blunder. "The handouts, if you please."

"There are handouts?" Brandt asks. "This is fascinating. Are there diagrams on these handouts?"

Caolan takes a stack of paper from Hagen and passes it to Alistair. "No. The diagrams are in my presentation." He sniffs, clearly not happy.

"For the love of god," Noah mutters, then adds, louder, "You can email everyone a copy, okay?"

The sulky frown disappears from Caolan's face. "Okay!"

There's a chance this may be getting out of Dáithí's and my control, but I can't make myself care when all my focus is needed to achieve my goal. I take the remaining handouts from Ari, keep one, and pass the few that are left to Dáithí, who glares at them like they're radioactive and hands them off as fast as he can.

Interesting... and concerning.

It only takes one glance to see what annoys Dáithí: the heading. I press my lips together to keep from laughing.

"Summit of Love: The Epic Challenge," Brandt reads, triggering a cascade of chuckles and chortles. "A Herculean trial to win the heart of an elf," he continues, and a snort manages to escape me.

Dáithí's elbow makes contact with my ribs. "Don't laugh," he hisses. "You'll encourage them."

I aim a skeptical glance around the table. The only people not laughing, aside from me and Dáithí, are Team Bro, who wear beatific smiles. "I think it's too late for that."

"What does 'herculean' mean?" Niamh asks. "I haven't heard that word before."

"Very powerful or difficult," Alistair explains. "Have you heard about the mythological Greek hero, Hercules?"

Niamh's face brightens. "Yes! He has some cameo appearances on *Xena: Warrior Princess.*"

I don't know what that is, but if it's connected to this challenge, maybe I need to watch it.

"Someone save me from the nineties," Noah mutters.

Alistair ignores him. "That's a great show! Hercules was, like, a demigod—the head god, Zeus, couldn't keep it in his pants, and Hercules happened one of those times. Though I think his name got changed, because sometimes people say Heracles. Anyway, a bunch of stuff happened, none of it good, and Hercules ended up being assigned twelve tasks—the Labors of Hercules—to make up for it. Or something. So we figured we could base Eoin's tasks on that."

"Loosely, though," Andrew adds. "Very loosely."

"Yeah." Hagen pulls a face. "There was a lot of slaying, capturing, and stealing on that list. We weren't on board with that."

"Neither am I," Raðulfr says.

I fold my arms and add, "Nor me." Unless it's that delivery guy who always flirts with Dáithí. I wouldn't *slay* him, exactly, but he might think I was going to. I side-eye Dáithí and wonder if that would make him mad. Does he like having the delivery guy's attention?

Ari's moved on, studying the paper. "There aren't twelve tasks on this list."

"Pfft." Alistair waves that off. "We did say it was *loosely* based."

Dáithí scoffs and mutters, "Yeah, loosely like they're both a bunch of tasks." He glances over at me and rolls his eyes, and the last of my anxiety settles.

"Okay, let's go through this," I declare, skimming over the list. It's not what I expected.

"Why do two of these only say 'redacted'?" Brandt asks before I can. "Is it a secret? Why? Most of us have the highest security clearance available. I want to know the secret."

"They've been redacted because Eoin knowing what they are will impact the outcome," Jared volunteers. "That's all."

I'm not sure I like the sound of that. "How am I supposed to complete them if I don't know what they are?"

"And how are we supposed to assess his completion of them if we don't know what they are?" Ari adds. He's found a pen somewhere and is making notes.

"Eoin's support team will be sent the complete list. We trust you not to betray the sanctity of your role by sharing it with him," Caolan informs him. "All I need is the names of everyone on Eoin's team."

"Me," Ari and Niamh say at the same time.

"You're on Dáithí's team?" Raðulfr asks Jared, who nods. "Then I'll be on Eoin's."

"I'm on Eoin's too." Brandt rubs his hands together. "And so is Steffen."

"What? No."

"Yes," Brandt insists, and when Steffen starts to protest, he adds, "I'll tell Dustin you're voluntarily joining in on a social activity so he stops nagging you about it."

Steffen stops arguing so sharply, it's as if the words were stolen from his mouth. "Fine."

"Great!" Alistair exclaims. "Who wants Team Success wristbands?" He holds up a handful of bright pink thick rubber bands, and hands go up around the table.

I watch in disbelief as they're passed around. "This is great for all of you, but I'm still worried about not knowing what those two tasks are." What if I never even start them? I can't do something if I don't know about its existence.

Hagen looks me in the eye across the table. "Trust me. It'll be fine. I'd never screw a bro over."

He wouldn't. Not when it comes to something this important. Stealing snack foods and almost setting the kitchen on fire, on the other hand, were things he used to do regularly.

"Dáithí means more to me than cupcakes," I remind him, just in case.

"I know," he replies, just as Dáithí says, "What?"

I pat his knee. "Don't worry about it. I'd never let him steal you."

"The list," Noah begs. "Please, can we stick to the list?"

With one last smile for Dáithí, I turn my attention back to the handout. Fine, I'll trust Hagen and not worry about the two redacted items. That leaves—

"Plan and execute a series of dates," Niamh reads. "Not gonna lie, this one's a disappointment. Don't they already go on dates? Along with everyone else who's interested in romance?"

"How many dates is 'a series'?" Ari asks.

Plan and execute. That's the key phrase for this task. Sure, Dáithí and I go on dates—out for dinner, to bars, to other places and events that interest us. The occasional theater production, concert, or movie. Whatever we're in the mood for at any given time. If I'm interpreting this task correctly, it isn't that. Aside from our first date—the one that didn't happen, and also the one to make up for it—we haven't been on any formal dates. After that first night together, Dáithí laid down his "casual" law, and we switched gears into what we have now.

So this task is about me knowing Dáithí, his likes and dislikes, and deliberately putting something together to show that.

I think.

"That's up to Eoin," Andrew is saying. "More than one, obviously, but otherwise it's completely his decision."

I grab Ari's pen and scrawl a note for myself. Dáithí's a social person, but he also likes structure and routine. It's part of what makes him so good at his job. If I planned half a dozen dates to take place over two weeks, he wouldn't be happy.

"Okay, next?" I ask. I think I've got a handle on the first one.

Ari protests. "I have questions—"

"No, you don't." I give him a warning look. Having a support team is one thing, and I'm grateful for it. Letting them take over isn't happening. "If questions come up, can I ask later?" I check.

"Of course." Dáithí answers before anyone else can. "Anytime."

"Then let's move on to the next task." I look back at the list. "Take a shift at Dáithí's job. Does that mean you wouldn't be there?" I ask him. "I'm not qualified to do your job."

He sucks in a little breath, and his eyes go soft.

"Awww," someone breathes, and when I turn, I see all four members of Team Bro grinning widely. Caolan writes something down.

"Huh?" Niamh asks, and Ari nods.

"What she said."

"We'll discuss it later," Jared tells them, but he and Noah are smiling too. I mentally replay what I said. There was nothing special there, but something caught their attention.

They wouldn't be smiling if it was a bad sign for me. One thing I've become sure of since this conversation began is that we're all on the same side and want the same outcome.

"Dáithí won't be there," Hagen says, "but you'll be given a training manual beforehand on basic processes and how the equipment works. You'll also have written instructions and access to another experienced receptionist if questions come up. Dáithí insisted." He directs the last part to Raðulfr and Brandt. "He didn't want to disrupt the office too much."

"Who cares?" Brandt proclaims. "This is more important than the office!"

The king sighs and shakes his head. "Thank you," he tells Dáithí.

"I don't understand how Eoin doing Dáithí's job for one day is going to prove his commitment." Steffen's frown is fierce.

I nod. "Yes. Could I have some context, please?"

Team Bro collectively shakes their heads. "No. Your team will be given the details they need for assessment, but no further context on this task is available to you," Caolan says. "Sorry."

Fuck. This is probably another of those situations where knowing details will impact my actions. I'm going to need to pay close attention in that training session—something they tell me will be what they assess me on. I scrawl another note.

"Okay, next... Clean Dáithí's apartment?" I turn to him. "Every week for the rest of our lives, or—"

"Just once for the assessment," he assures me, and I shrug. "Done."

"This list is nothing like what I expected," Ari mutters, taking his pen back to write something down.

"This last one is interesting," Raðulfr muses. "Surprise Dáithí."

Interesting isn't the word I'd choose. "As in... buy him a gift? Or leap out of the closet yelling?"

"No further context on this task is available to you," Caolan informs me. That probably means that the decision I make about what constitutes a surprise is as much a factor in assessment as the surprise itself. Some of my earlier anxiety comes back.

I exhale deeply and nod. "Thank you. I can work with this." Ari's not the only one who wasn't expecting a list like this, but at least it's not an impossible open-ended task, like moving every grain of sand on a beach. These seem to be targeted, and while I could opt to take as long as I want with them, I could also finish them within a week if I chose.

The ones I know about, anyway.

It's fine. I've got this. I'm going to prove to Dáithí that our happy ever after is inevitable.

CHAPTER TWELVE

Dáithí

THE CALM WAY Eoin handled the list—I refuse to call it the Summit of Love, no matter how much Alistair begs—is still weighing on my mind when I get home. Leaving the door ajar for Eoin, who's parking his car out front even though I suggested that he might want to be alone tonight to think about everything, I walk over to my couch and belly flop onto it.

Tonight was... surreal. I grew up in a community with a lot of dragons, and obviously I've spent a lot of time with them since I started working for the king, so I'm used to dealing with situations that are hard to explain, but I've never been at the center of one.

My nose is smashed against a throw pillow, but that doesn't stop me from sucking in a deep, fabric-scented breath. Hm. I might need to wash the covers on my pillows.

Maybe Eoin will do it when he cleans my place.

Groaning, I bury my face deeper into the pillow. Some of the tasks on the list might seem nonsensical, but they've all been carefully picked for reasons I had to agree with. Even the two that were redacted—putting Eoin into a situation where he has to help me take care of a living entity, and leaving something important to me in his care—have logic and reason behind them. These aren't pass/fail tasks; they're designed to showcase Eoin's commitment to me, or lack thereof. The scale for assessing them is broad, and having others weigh in will give me perspectives I might not have considered.

But was Eoin taking everything in stride because he's confident, or because he doesn't care? He barely even asked any questions. Was that a sign that he's willing to take on anything for me, or that he'd be willing to walk away if the tests are too much?

Distant footsteps reach my ears, and a moment later, I hear the front door close and the sound of the lock engaging. Eoin's here. That's a sign, isn't it? If he was ready to walk away, or thinking about it, he wouldn't have insisted on coming over tonight. There wouldn't have been those few moments around the king's table where we connected, the awkwardness of this scenario falling away, replaced by the comfort of *us*.

"Is this a new thing?" he asks now, amusement lacing his voice. "I can't tell if you're having a tantrum or trying to tempt me. If it's the latter, it normally works better without pants."

A reluctant snort of laughter escapes me, and I roll over to look up at him. There's soft fondness on his face and humor in his eyes. "Are you saying I don't tempt you with my pants on?"

Heat replaces humor. "Honey, you tempt me by breathing."

Oh. I go from tired and insecure to feeling like a sex god in seconds. Eoin's the only one who's ever thought of me that way. I don't doubt my own appeal—I'm too old and have done too much with too many people for that kind of insecurity—but somehow I'm special when I'm with Eoin.

I reach an arm up for him, and he takes my hand and kisses the palm, then nudges my hip with his knee. "Scoot over."

Once we're wrapped together on the too-small couch and I have the length of him pressed against me, his legs tangled with mine, it's easier to relax. Maybe it's foolish of me to get this attached; maybe he will move on. Maybe that's going to be soon, now that I've given him that stupid list. None of that matters right now.

Still... "Sorry tonight got so out of hand," I mutter against his neck. His arms tighten around me.

"The out-of-hand part was my favorite part," he says, kissing my hair. "Before that I was freaking out that you'd change your mind and just end things after all."

Oh.

I've spent way too much of the past twenty-four hours feeling like a terrible person. I don't like it.

"Eoin—"

"Stop. No guilt, please. This is what I want, remember?"

"But—"

"No. Dáithí, seriously, I want to do this. I'm going to win your trust along with your heart, and for the rest of our lives, every time we have an argument or you start to feel a little neglected because I'm busy with work, you'll be able to remember this. Not that I'd ever let you feel neglected," he adds, and I huff a reluctant little laugh.

"You know I think you're amazing, right?" I check. He can read me like a book, but I'm not always so sure about what he's feeling.

"I never doubted it," he assures me. "Trust me, Dáithí. Trust me to prove how perfect we are for each other."

My chest tightens, and I force myself to breathe deeply

and evenly. I want to tell him I do, but my brain won't let me speak those words. "I trust you to try," I finally say instead, and he kisses my hair again.

"That's enough for me—for now, anyway. We don't have to talk about this, though. We'll be spending enough time and effort on it over the next few months. Tell me about the rest of your day."

Few months? I guess that's a good sign for me, if he's not planning to cram everything into the next week or so. But he's right; we don't need to spend all our time together talking about this.

"My day? Not that exciting. The usual dramas with people not being able to read the instructions for the printer. I'd rather hear what's going on with this hockey thing." I was so preoccupied yesterday that I never asked.

"The meeting with the marketing guy from the Warhammers?" Eoin asks.

"Yeah. Erik."

"Do you know him?" Eoin's surprise is clear. "You didn't mention it."

I shrug. "No, I've never met him before. I remember his name because his nervous babbling about the meeting was so sweet."

He stiffens slightly against me, but not in the good way. "Sweet, huh?"

"Sure." I'm ignoring the implied jealousy. We have enough going on in our relationship without adding that to the mix, and he's got nothing to be jealous about anyway. "So... what was the meeting about?"

It takes another three seconds for him to relax, and then he says, "Hockey. The team reached out to us last season—ironically, right before the king met Jared. An elf—that's your friend Erik—was their new head of marketing, and he thought having the king attend some games might interest more elves in the sport. We hadn't gotten any further than me setting up a meeting with the league's security people when that night at the hockey game happened, and obviously it became a low priority after that."

Since the king was busy having his whole relationship with Jared derailed, yeah, his priorities definitely got shaken up. And then I guess the season ended, since ice hockey is a winter sport... right? Or do they play year-round, since the games are inside?

"When does the new season start?" I ask. Eoin said the team got in contact *last* season, so that would mean they're either currently playing a season or one will start soon. His answer to my question should tell me which it is.

"October, according to Erik." There's a thread of laughter in his voice that tells me he's not fooled by my genius. "The players start training camp next month, and Erik wants the king and Jared to visit for a photo opportunity."

"Really?" That doesn't seem like a productive use of training time. "What did the king say?"

Eoin laughs. "That Jared thinks the Glaives are a better team."

I sit up, ignoring his "Ouch!" as my knee jabs him in the thigh. "Shut up! He didn't say that."

Hoisting himself upright more carefully than I did, he says, "He did. There are pictures from that game with Jared wearing a Glaives jersey, so it wasn't a surprise. But apparently Jared somehow met one of the Warhammers' players, so he's fine with showing support for the team anyway."

Clearly Jared and I need to have lunch again. Just because I'm not interested in a sport doesn't mean I'm not interested in gossip surrounding that sport. When did he meet a Community Hockey League player?

"That's all? Just a photo during training?" I'm so let down.

Leaning sideways and propping his elbow on the back of

the couch, Eoin says, "No, they're going to attend some games as well. Jared really does like hockey. *Erik* was thrilled with the commitment they made—four games during the regular season, then every local game during the playoffs."

"If the team—Warhammers, right?"

"Yes."

"If the Warhammers even make the playoffs."

Absently—his attention on... my ear? My hair?—he replies, "No, they will. The league's only got four teams—the Warhammers are based here, the Glaives are headquartered in the South, and the Morningstars and Battleaxes are out west. All four teams play the regular season and then the playoffs."

Laughter spills from me. "Seriously? What's the point of even having playoffs if it's the same teams? Just base the season's winner on the total points or something."

He's smiling, but it still seems like he's not paying attention, and that's confirmed when he reaches out and brushes his thumb against my earlobe. "Your skin is so soft here," he murmurs when I shiver. "So sensitive."

I snap my fingers in front of his face, and his attention is immediately on me.

"Rude," he chides, but that smile widens.

"So is zoning out during a conversation. Sex later—talk now." But I lean in and press a kiss to the hinge of his jaw, just so he knows sex is definitely happening later.

"Fine. There's not much else to say, though. Erik's assured me that a private suite will be made available for the king, even though you and I both know Raðulfr will go wandering through the crowd if he gets a chance, anyway."

"Heh. Yeah. Especially if there are elves in it."

Eoin shrugs. "Exactly. The only other thing that concerns me is the training camp, since he'll potentially be up close with anyone who's there. I've asked Erik for a list of everyone scheduled to attend, including support staff, and I'll get someone to check them all for prior incidents or affiliations that might concern us—the usual procedure."

I've heard everyone on Eoin's team—including him—complain about having to run background checks often enough to know they all think it's boring. He usually assigns it to whoever's pissed him off the most that week. "Are you going to get Niamh to do it?"

"No," he says, surprising me. "I thought I'd give it to Ari."

"*Ari?*" His second-in-command and the closest friend he has on the team? I sense an interesting tidbit of gossip. "Why?"

"I'm not sure, honestly. Instinct. I just feel like it's something I should get Ari to do." He screws up his face. "He'll make my life hell for it."

"Fuck, yeah." I don't question the decision, though. It's one of the things I've noticed a lot, working with the Earth species for the past decade or so—they look for logic and reason to make their decisions, and often talk themselves out of their instinctive reactions. We elves are the opposite. Instinct is the first factor we consider, logic coming second and often not included at all, if our instinctive reaction is strong enough. In a case like this, where Ari is perfectly qualified and suitable to do the job, Eoin wouldn't have bothered to rationalize his decision—there's no need. "Can I be there when you tell him?"

Eoin's lips quirk. "I thought you liked Ari."

"What's that got to do with anything?"

CHAPTER THIRTEEN

Eoin

I LEAVE Dáithí at reception with one last kiss and head for my office, grateful for the quiet before most people arrive. He wanted to come in earlier than usual so he could clear some things that didn't get attended to yesterday, and I decided to come with him and get a head start on the Summit of Love Challenge.

Dáithí *hates* that name. I thought it was ridiculous, in a catchy kind of way, but he got all fired up this morning when I mentioned it, which led to me apologizing profusely with a blowjob. I've made a mental note to tease him with it as often as possible, just so I need to apologize some more.

The office is empty still, so I aim a spell at the light switch on my way through the darkness to my desk. I had coffee with Dáithí earlier, but I wouldn't mind a cup of tea—later. If I go to the breakroom now, there's a chance I'll be waylaid or distracted. I want to spend some time on the challenge before I start on my work for the day.

Some of the tasks will have to wait for a more appropriate time—like taking Dáithí's shift, which needs to be planned for an appropriate time, or cleaning his apartment. I check my calendar and make a note to see if he's got anything planned for Saturday morning. Maybe I can convince him to go out for brunch or do some shopping—or both. I make a note to ask Jared and the king what they're doing too. They could keep him company while I'm scrubbing his kitchen floor.

That raises another question—do I need to do the cleaning manually, or can I use my magic? Since the tasks aren't designed to be tricks, I'm assuming the list would specify if I couldn't, but I'll check anyway.

I can't plan for the two tasks that were redacted, so I focus instead on the date planning and the surprise, making lists of ideas.

My list of questions has gotten a lot longer when a notebook thumps onto my desk beside my hand, and I become aware that some of my team have arrived.

"What's that for?" I ask, not bothering to glance up. I have a sentence to finish.

"Things I thought of since I saw you last night," Ari replies, pulling his chair over from his desk and sitting down. That stupid pink wristband is still on his arm. "Caolan sent me the full list and the criteria for assessment, which I had to swear not to disclose. So I won't."

"I don't want you to." I reach for the notebook. "I'm going to do this fairly." The first page is a list of questions that looks a lot like mine. He has a couple I hadn't thought of, probably because he has more context than I do. "Thank you for this." It almost makes me feel bad that I'm going to stick him with the background checks on the Warhammers.

He shrugs. "I'm on your support team, remember? I also started a list of ideas for your dates and things that might come up while you're working reception, so you can be prepared."

"I hadn't gotten to that last one yet, but I've been working on the dates too." I flip to what looks like the right page and skim through his list. "No to camping—Dáithí doesn't like it."

"What? But he used to talk about camping at Rothschen River. He used to go all the time."

I nod. "Yes, but that was back home. He'd sacrifice hot water and a comfortable mattress because he loved it so much, but he's not willing to do that here. He says it still reminds him too much of what he's lost."

Ari's face falls. "Oh. Yeah, I…" He doesn't bother to finish, but he doesn't need to. We both understand Dáithí's perspective.

"He recently started hiking again, though," I volunteer. "Maybe he'll eventually want to camp again too." I know he will—it's not in us elves to stay separate from nature for long, and Dáithí doesn't get enough time away from the city to forgo camping forever.

"Time heals," Ari says quietly with a sad smile. "We have enough of it now that we can let it take its course."

I pat his arm wordlessly, and we both pull ourselves away from melancholy thoughts. He's right—we have time now.

"What have you come up with so far for date ideas?" he asks. "How many are you planning?"

I push the list I've been making toward him. "Three to start with. I might add some more later, though."

He reads my notes, a faint crease forming between his brows at one point, only to be replaced by a smile. "This one first," he says, tapping the paper. "I wouldn't have thought of it, but it's very Dáithí. Can you pull it off?"

"Maybe. I need to make some calls and ask for favors, but if I activate the friend tree, it should be possible."

"I'll leave you to it, then. Anything I can do as a member of your support team?"

"No—actually, yes." I grab his notebook, flip back to the

first page, and add a few of my own questions to the bottom. "Could you check with the Bros and Dáithí and get the answers to some of these?" I check it against my list, making sure everything is covered, then hold it out to him.

"No problem." He takes the notebook and stands, grabbing the back of his chair in preparation to go back to his desk.

"I'm also sending you some stuff to follow up from the hockey meeting Raðulfr and I had the other day with Caolan."

Ari freezes. "What kind of stuff?"

I grimace, and his groan is loud enough to attract attention from some of the other members of the security team. "Eoin, noooo. It's not my turn."

The curious faces that were looking our way immediately turn back to what they were doing. Brayan actually leaves the office, as if that would stop me from assigning something to him if I wanted to.

"I know, but it has to be you this time. I'm sorry."

He doesn't reply, just sighs and glares at me as he shoves his chair toward his desk—hard. It crashes, and he narrows his eyes as if to say he wishes it was me.

Smirking, I ask, "Feel better?"

While he stomps out of the office, notebook in hand, I email him the list of names from Warhammers Erik, check my emails for anything urgent, then grab my phone. Time to see if I can set up this date.

It rings out the first time, no voicemail, but with this person, that means nothing. He misplaces his phone all the time, and he disabled voicemail when he realized people expected him to check it and return their calls. I try again... and then again.

Finally, on the fifth ring of the fourth call, it connects. "Hm?"

Crap. This is obviously not the best time. "Fabian, it's Eoin."

"Hm."

Dammit. "Fabian?"

"Hello?" he sounds startled, as though he wasn't expecting anyone to be talking to him. Good—that means he's listening.

"Hi, Fabian. It's Eoin—from King Raðulfr's security team." We don't know each other all that well, and he can be vague at the best of times.

"Oh—hello. Did I call you about something? I don't remember what I needed, but I can check my notes."

I grin. "No, I called you. I have a very big favor to ask of you... well, of your boyfriend, really."

"Rhys? What kind of favor? Did you join his study? I promise, your personal information is very private—he doesn't even know himself who's generating the data. Except for mine, of course."

Considering that Rhys is running a scientific study on the effects sex has on metaphysical health, I *hope* everyone's information is private. "No, that's not—"

"You didn't join the study?" Fabian's voice is full of disappointment. "Oh, Eoin—you of all people must know how important this is. You were at the meeting with the king when we—"

"I joined the study, Fabian, but that's not what I need to talk to Rhys about." I interrupt before he can get more off track and take me with him.

He pauses. "Oh. You know he and I are exclusive, right? He won't go on a date with you."

I take a deep breath and cling to my patience. "I wasn't going to ask him. I'm hoping he can help with the arrangements for me to take someone else on a date."

The gasp of excitement is my only warning before I'm hit

with a barrage of questions. "A date? Who? Is it a first date? Do you love them? How did you meet? What can Rhys do to help? Is—"

"Fabian!"

He stops. "You can answer those questions first while I think of some more."

How generous. "It's Dáithí, Fabian. I've been seeing Dáithí since March last year, remember?"

"My Dáithí?"

"I prefer to think of him as *mine*."

"You're the commitment-phobe!"

I tip my head back and squeeze my eyes shut. This isn't a positive start. "Actually, I'm trying to convince Dáithí of the opposite, so—"

"The Summit of Love is for you!"

If he yells one more annoying declaration in my ear, I'm hanging up and finding another way to get his boyfriend's number. Brandt will have it.

Fuck. I should have just asked Brandt to begin with. He's on my support team—a sentence I never thought would exist.

"How do you even know about that?" I demand.

"So it *is* you? Caolan told me about it. He had to check something in the archive while he and his bros were planning the tasks. This is so exciting! Do you need Rhys's help to sweep Dáithí off his feet? I can help too! Rhys and I are both very romantic." He pauses. "In different ways, though."

"Could I have Rhys's phone number?" This is going nowhere fast.

"Sure, but... aren't you going to tell me why?" I can practically hear Fabian's pout, and I silently promise myself that I'll funnel the next favor I need through my support group. They can deal with the overeager dragons.

"I'm in a hurry," I say. "But Rhys can tell you all about it, I promise. I'll let him know he has my permission."

With a big sigh to convey how unhappy he is with me, he gives me Rhys's number, then says, "I'm setting an alarm to call him in half an hour, so you better be finished by then."

Great.

I've only met Rhys a few times, but he's definitely the more settled member of that relationship. This next call is guaranteed to be easier... I hope.

"Rhys Griffiths," he answers, and I exhale in relief. That's already better.

"Hi, Rhys. This is Eoin Feirstrigh. We met—"

"Hello, Eoin. Of course I remember you. How are you?" There's a tiny note of concern in the question, and I smile wryly to myself.

"I guess Fabian told you about the challenge."

There's a tiny pause, and then he answers, "I think so. He called it the Summit of Love."

It seems like that name's going to catch on, dammit. "I want to go on record as saying that I knew nothing about the name. I'm pretty sure Dáithí didn't approve it either."

He snorts. "Well, if you have Hagen, Caolan, and their friends helping, there are probably going to be a bunch of things that spin out of control."

"I'm expecting it. Anyway, since you already know about the challenge, that's going to save me giving you background. One of the tasks is to plan some dates, and I was hoping you could help."

"Me?" His surprise is audible. "I'm not great with that sort of thing. Scientist, remember?"

"Fabian seems to think you're romantic, but I've got the idea part handled. It's the execution I need a favor for." A big one.

"I'm intrigued. What do you need? If it's in my power, I'll do it—if only to make Fabian happy."

That's sweet—and I completely understand his motive.

There's a lot I'd do to make Dáithí smile, too. "I'm not sure if you remember, but last time we met, you mentioned that your company has a suite for the baseball season—that you had to go once to chat up potential investors."

Rhys groans. "Yes. I still don't know why I had to go. Nobody wanted to talk about our research—it was just bragging and gossip the whole time, with the occasional comment about baseball. And half of those were about the players' personal lives, or how they looked in their pants."

Perfect. Dáithí loves gossip *and* baseball pants on other people. "That's how I remember you describing it. Is there any chance you can talk your boss into including me and Dáithí on the guestlist? I'm willing to make a donation." Not as big as what the people who are usually invited can give, but money's money, right? I earn decent money and I'm not a wild spender.

"Don't worry about that," Rhys says. "The DEA is a backer of my research, remember? You work for the DEA—directly for the king—so you qualify as a representative. Leave it with me and I'll get you on the list. Which game do you want to go to?"

"Uh..." I can't believe it was that easy. I thought for sure I'd need to talk him into it, maybe talk to his boss as well. Definitely throw some cash at the company. "There's a home game this weekend, but if that's not possible, whenever the next one is." I'll make the scheduling work.

"I'll call you back later today to confirm when, but you can consider this done, Eoin."

And just like that, the details for the first task fall into place.

CHAPTER FOURTEEN

Dáithí

It's not until midmorning that Hagen sidles up to my desk. I side-eye him. Neither of us is stupid—he knows I know he deliberately waited for the lull so I can't avoid him.

"What?"

He pouts. "Is that any way to talk to a member of your support team? I could have been on Eoin's, you know. I've known him longer."

"You're welcome to change teams," I offer. Truthfully, I'm not sure if I mean it. This whole thing might have turned into something bigger than I was expecting, and I definitely don't feel like I'm in control anymore, but it's nice knowing there are people who care. It's *really* nice knowing Eoin might have a chance to—

No. Nope. Not going there.

Hagen's giving me his best offended look, so I sigh and admit, "I wish you wouldn't, though. Your help has been... helpful." That's the best I can do. I'm known for snark and sass, not kind words.

He either doesn't care that I'm not a wordsmith or knows that he's not getting anything better out of me, because the offense turns to smiles. "Great! Anyway, I'm here on business."

I perk up. "Actual business? Do I need to schedule the conference room for you? Or order catering?"

"No, no... Summit of Love business."

Wincing, I glance around. "Could we not call it that at the office? Or ever?"

"I don't know why you're so precious about this. It's a great name. The commemorative plaque we're having made for Eoin if he wins is going to be gorgeous."

"The what?" He's joking, right?

"Don't worry about that for now. We've got it handled."

I'm not reassured at all, and add "commemorative plaque" to my mental list of things to ask Noah to forbid. He's got more practice dealing with them. "Either change the name, or stop using it at the office. Your call."

"But—"

I pick up my spray bottle—the red one.

"Okay! Fine. Sheesh. I won't use the name when I'm talking to you here. I don't know what your issue with it is, though. It's not like you made any suggestions."

Biting my tongue to keep from saying we didn't need a fucking name to begin with, because that would just mean engaging with him, I set the bottle down. "What do you need, Hagen?"

He looks like he wants to argue some more about the name, but I narrow my eyes and he changes his mind. Instead, he leans against the high part of the desk and says, "You said you wanted to handle the two redacted tasks yourself. Have you decided what to do yet?"

"It hasn't even been a day," I point out, avoiding any mention of the fact that I deliberately have *not* thought about it.

Hagen seems to know anyway, because he nods, smirking.

"Yeah, I figured. I'm going to email you a list of suggestions we put together."

"When?" I demand, exasperated. "When did you have time to do that in the past thirteen hours while also sleeping and working?"

"We multitasked."

"While *sleeping*?"

He shrugs. "It's a gift."

Would anyone notice if he went missing? Probably. Would they care enough to do anything about it?

Something on my face must give away my thoughts, because he straightens hurriedly and takes a step back. "Jaid would never rest if something happened to me, Dáithí."

His boyfriend would probably send me a thank-you letter, but all I say is, "I don't know what you're talking about. Was there something else?"

He's eyeing me suspiciously now, and I give him my sweetest smile, the one guaranteed to terrify anyone who knows—and has crossed—me.

"Nope. Not while you have your scary face on." He turns away, hesitates, and turns back. "Just remember that Eoin will need time for both those tasks. You need to get them started as soon as possible."

I hold out until he's almost at the security gate before I cave. "Hagen, come back." To his credit, he's not gloating when he rejoins me. "What were your suggestions?"

"We've asked around—quietly—and have the names of some people who'd let you pet-sit, to see how Eoin copes with having to help you look after a living creature. You've got your choice of two cats, three dogs, and a parakeet. Alistair's also in talks with someone about their seahorse. It's apparently very needy, which would be a great test, but the tank is too big to move. We're not sure if it's a feasible option."

"Seahorse?" It takes me a moment to place what that is—my mind goes immediately to land horses, but they would need super big tanks. "I don't think I've ever even seen a picture of a seahorse." Or if I did, I didn't know what I was looking at. "People keep them as pets?"

Hagen shrugs again. "I don't think it's common, but I guess so. They don't look like horses at all, though. I asked Jaid why they're called seahorses, but he didn't know."

I scribble *seahorse* on the blotter beside my keyboard as a reminder to google it later. "What else is on the list, other than pet-sitting?"

He hesitates. "Pet-sitting might be the best option."

"Hagen."

"You could babysit for a weekend. That might be trickier, though, because so far nobody's volunteered their kids for a whole weekend. One guy in the legal department at CSG said he'd pay you to take over coaching his kid's soccer team, but that's not what we're looking for."

"I'm not babysitting kids that don't know me for a whole weekend," I declare flatly. I rarely want to look after kids for more than a couple of hours, even when they *do* know me—and more to the point, I know they're not going to turn into monsters as soon as their parents leave. Other people's children are precious as long as those other people are around.

The coaching, on the other hand... Hagen's right, it's not what we're looking for, but it could fit the "care for something important" task. Maybe. If I convince Eoin I care about coaching a kids' soccer team.

It might help if I knew more about soccer than what the uniforms look like.

"Well, then it's pet-sitting or getting your own pet, which is a huge decision and not something to be done just for the challenge."

"Huh? Oh, right. Of course. I'd never get a pet just for the sake of the challenge." As always when I think about getting a pet, I remember with fond sadness the ones I loved. I've outlived a lot of precious animal companions in my life, and I miss them all. The grief over losing them fades until the happy memories are stronger, but it never completely disappears.

It's been a long time since I had a pet, though. Embla died not long after we realized the anomalies were a problem, and even after I'd mourned her passing, I didn't want to get another pet with everything so unstable. It's been thousands of years.

Maybe...

"Dáithí?"

I look up and see Hagen still standing there, waiting for me to say something. I have no idea if he asked me a question or just wants me to tell him which option I've decided on.

"Let me think about it," I say. "I'll try to make a decision today. Or maybe tomorrow."

He nods slowly. "Are you okay? I didn't mean to upset you."

"I'm fine. Just thinking about some of the pets I've had." I muster a smile. "You know how it is."

"Hard. It's hard to lose anyone you love. I have to get back to work, but you can call any of us if you have questions or need help. Eoin already sent Ari to ask us a bunch of stuff. He's taking this seriously, Dáithí."

I wait for hope to rise, like it always does when I think Eoin might actually prove himself, then realize it doesn't have to—its new resting place is so much closer to my conscious self than it was before. When did that happen, and how much more will it hurt if things don't turn out? "I know he is."

Hagen gives me one last, long look before wandering off

toward the security gate. I wait until he's through it before flopping back in my chair. So much to think about.

Starting with, am I ready for another pet? I've been here on Earth, safe from the threat of destruction, for over a decade. I have a home, a secure job, and it's been *so long* since I had an animal companion to love. Maybe it's time to consider it.

A LITTLE OVER twenty-seven hours later, I'm convinced I've made the right decision, but cursing myself for choosing a two-bedroom townhome with a courtyard instead of a house with a yard. After all, if I'm going to adopt all these precious babies, I'll need space for them.

Jared chooses that moment to say, "One, Dáithí. You know it wouldn't be fair to get more than one, at least at first."

I look around the shelter he brought me to when I asked for his advice on adopting a pet here on Earth, and reluctantly concede that he has a point. "Fine. I don't have room for them all anyway. Explain to me how this works—I choose my baby and take them home?"

He shakes his head, grinning. "Not exactly. You choose your baby, then fill out a dozen forms and pay a fee. The shelter will take forty-eight business hours to do a background check on you, make sure you're not someone who has a history of violence against animals or has had a neglected pet in the past." His eyes widen, and he lowers his voice. "Is that going to be a problem? With your, um, migration history?"

It takes me a moment to understand he's concerned about my fake identity being discovered—because of course I wasn't born in this country, or even in this universe, so all my documents are technically fake. "No, it's fine," I assure him. They're good fakes—the kind that are registered on government databases as real.

Relieved, he says, "Good. Okay, so after the background check comes back, they'll call you, and you'll get to come pick up your baby—and do more paperwork, plus pay another fee for the adoption."

"The forty-eight-hour delay is for your benefit, as well," a voice says, and we turn to see the volunteer who walked us in approaching. She was called away a few minutes ago to help with an unsettled dog. "It acts as a cooling-off period. A lot of people decide to get a pet on impulse, but then change their minds when they've had time to think about it."

"That's sensible," I approve. "Pet ownership isn't a game."

She eyes me curiously. "You've had pets before?"

"Oh, yes. Not for—" I cough to cover my almost slip. "Excuse me. Not for a while, but I had several while I was... growing up." That's probably the best answer I'm going to come up with. I hope she doesn't ask what kind, because then I'll have to outright lie.

To my relief, her face turns sympathetic. "It's hard to lose them, isn't it? I'm glad you're ready to share your love again. Did you want a dog?" She glances at the enclosures around us, which all seem to contain dogs. "How much space do you have?"

"Not much," I say regretfully. "My work hours are fairly regular, but I don't think a big dog would be a good idea—they'd be cooped up all day."

That wins me a nod of approval. "You're at work all day, then? Is there anyone else at home?"

I shake my head. "Just me."

Grimacing, she glances around at the dogs again. "Honestly, I don't think we have any dogs at the moment that would suit you. As you can see, most of them are big, and the few smaller ones we have are young and energetic. They might not need as much space as a big dog, but they'd still feel cooped up and lonely while you were at work." She shrugs. "If you're set on a dog, maybe check back next week? We do get older dogs quite often when their people pass on and there's no one to take them."

"Maybe," I muse. "Let's have a look around the other animals and see if I fall in love with anyone before I decide."

"What about a cat?" Jared suggests as we leave the dog room and enter another. "Margie misses me when I'm at work, but she's never upset about being alone."

"We do have some cats who might suit…"

I'm not sure what she says after that, because I've stopped listening. My attention has been caught by the sweetest face I've ever seen. "It's a bunny," I whisper, leaning forward to see that twitchy little nose better. At least, I think it's a bunny. For some reason, the bunnies that appear most often in media are anthropomorphized.

"Dáithí?" Jared appears at my side. "We lost you. Ohhhhh."

"Have you ever had a pet rabbit before?" the volunteer, who never told us her name, asks.

I shake my head. "No, never."

"Okay, well… this lady would actually be pretty perfect for you. Rabbits can live for about twelve years, and she's three, which means she's past her toddler years. She's also very placid, even for her breed, and she's the perfect example of how her species have more energy in the morning and evening. So while you're at work, she'll probably be perfectly fine napping and having quiet time." She flips the latch on the enclosure and reaches in to pick up my new sweetheart. "Want to hold her?"

I already have my hands out when she turns, and I pay close attention to her instructions. Soon I have the sweetest, softest bundle of brown and white fur cuddled up to me, that nose twitching up at me as though asking me to keep her.

"Is she healthy?" Jared asks. I don't care, but I listen to the answer anyway, in case my new baby needs medical assistance.

"Perfectly. She's been desexed and had all her shots and been microchipped. She was a little girl's birthday present, but it turned out the little girl was severely allergic. They had to call an ambulance when she went into anaphylactic shock. Not a fun birthday for her."

"That poor girl—both of them," Jared says, running a finger down my bunny's back.

"When her father brought this lady in, he said she'd made him promise that we'd call to let her know if new people adopted her. I hope that would be okay with you?"

"Of course," I murmur. "We can send her a photo, too, if she'd like."

"That's very kind. Thank you." She hesitates. "Normally at this point I'm supposed to ask if you'd like to meet any of the other animals, but..."

"Nope. This sweetheart is for me. Did her previous owner have the chance to give her a name?"

"No, I'm afraid."

I smile as my sweetheart closes her eyes and tucks her face against my chest. "Then her name is Elsking."

CHAPTER FIFTEEN

Eoin

My phone chimes just as I'm sitting down with Ari to go over what he learned from the Warhammers' background checks, and I glance at it just to make sure it's not work-related.

"Instant smile. It's from Dáithí, then," Ari teases, and my cheeks get hot.

"Yeah." I shove it into my pocket without opening the message. It can wait until after the meeting.

Ari scoffs. "Just read it, Eoin. I don't care."

Part of me wants to hold out on principle, but that's just stupid.

> Are you free after work tonight? I need you
> to come somewhere with me and then portal
> me home.

I reread the message twice. This is the first time Dáithí's asked me to portal him—he's come with me before, of course, but he's never asked me to as a favor. I mentioned it once and he said I'm not his personal transport service. Plus, he likes taking public transport so he can people watch.

"Is he okay?" Ari asks in concern as I just stare at my phone.

"Yeah. At least, I think so." I show him the text, and he shrugs.

"Maybe he's going on a shopping spree and doesn't want to carry the bags home? Or he's buying furniture."

That's possible. "He did say a couple of times that he wants a new rug for his bedroom."

"There you go. Rugs can be awkward to carry."

I make a sound of agreement, then text Dáithí back with an affirmative. We haven't had any time to spend together in the past couple of days. The viceroy who looks after the elves in Romania went into early labor with her baby, and I went with Raðulfr so he could manage things there until a temporary replacement was found. I also spent several hours hovering outside the birthing room, grateful that Raðulfr and the viceroy didn't require my presence inside.

I got home late last night, and of course he was at his place. We got ten minutes together this morning when I got to work, but he's promised to stay at my—

> Thank you! And can we stay at mine tonight instead of yours?

Correction, he's asked me to stay with him tonight.

> Sure. Come find me when you're done for the day.

I have a list as long as my arm of things to catch up with, so I'm bringing some work home to deal with while Dáithí watches TV or after he's asleep. At least that way I still get to spend the evening with him, instead of hanging around here alone.

When I finally put my phone down, Ari's watching me.

"He makes you happy, doesn't he? Not just 'life is good' happy, but happy down to your bones."

I smile. "Yeah. I want to do the same for him too."

"You will. Whatever scared him that's holding him back, he'll get through it, and then you can be happy together." There's an edge of something in his face... not sadness. Wistfulness? Is Ari a closet romantic?

Or is he lonely?

Because a quiet word to Dáithí is all it would take for him to start hunting down a match for Ari. He likes Ari and *loves* matchmaking. It would be like giving him a present.

Hmm.

Ari's words fully sink in a second later. "Wait, what do you mean, whatever scared him? You think Dáithí had a bad experience or something?" Wouldn't he have told me if that was the case? We've both been open about our pasts... I thought.

"You *don't* think he did?" Ari sounds astonished. "I assumed that had to be part of it. I mean, sure, your reputation with relationships sucks, but you and he have been exclusive for over a year. Why is he still so sure you'll want to walk away? So much so that he wasn't even willing to try until you forced him to?"

My mouth is hanging open. I can't believe I never put that together before—I had all the pieces, even asked the same questions Ari just gave voice to. "Well, fuck."

Ari pats my shoulder. "It's okay. Now, most—"

"It's *not* okay. For starters, whatever hurt him must have been bad. Bad enough that he never even mentioned it, just let the wounds fester."

"Maybe don't use that word if you talk to him about it."

"Is this a sign that he's not that invested in me? Don't people talk about their past wounds with the people they love? Did I ever have a chance at all, if whatever happened is so bad, he can't even talk about it?"

"I guess the Warhammers are going to have to wait. Eoin, listen—you're blowing this out of proportion. We don't even know for sure that something *did* hurt Dáithí. What do I know about stuff like this? And even if his heart was broken or whatever, the fact that he's willing to let you try says a lot about how he feels about you. Don't get in your head over this."

Sucking in a deep breath through my nose, I hold it, then exhale slowly. I hate when he's right. There's nothing I can do about this except what I was already doing.

There's just one last painful thought I need to shake. "What if I objectively pass all the tests but his past hurt is still too much for him to get over?"

Ari grimaces. "Then you might have to give him the space he needs to heal. Or... have you ever asked the king if you and Dáithí are paired souls?"

I shake my head before he's even finished asking the question. "It doesn't matter to me. I love Dáithí, even if there is a chance our paths will diverge—" I freeze. Fuck. "That would be dirty play, Ari. Dáithí and I agreed that this is how I'll prove myself."

"I'm not suggesting that you should renege. But if, like you said, you objectively pass all the tests and Dáithí is still struggling to let go of his fear, that could be an ace up your sleeve... if you're paired souls. He won't have to worry about you not wanting a committed relationship if your souls are guaranteed to grow in the same direction, because if that happens, he'll feel the same way."

"It's not going to happen," I say reflexively, but I can't deny the temptation in his plan. The only potential downside is that Raðulfr might say we're *not* paired souls, and then I'd be right back at square one, only with a secret from Dáithí that might be unethical to keep. "It's a worry for another day," I add finally. "Let me prove myself first. It might not even be a problem."

"Exactly." Ari studies my face, then nods like he's satisfied with whatever he saw there. "Ready to hear about the Warhammers?"

"That depends on whether I'm going to like what you say."

He shrugs. "Mostly. A few drunk and disorderlies from after the playoffs final three years ago. Two public indecencies—the enforcement reports on those were pretty clear, and I don't think they need to be followed up. One guy and his girlfriend decided to get frisky in a park, but it was late at night and nobody was around except for one guy walking his dog."

I wave that off. Sex with a partner isn't going to pose a threat to Raðulfr, even if they decide to do it at center ice. "The other one?"

Ari snorts. "Guy had to pee real bad and couldn't find a bathroom. He thought the alley was safe."

"But it wasn't. Poor guy." That's not a concern either. "So we're clear?"

"No. There's one player who was charged with aggravated assault and destruction of private property. The assault charge didn't stick, both because they couldn't prove intent and the doorbell camera clearly showed that he was swinging at the window and the victim jumped in the way, but I think we need to ask some questions."

I hold out my hand, and without asking what I want, Ari passes me the enforcement report. Skimming the list of property damage, I let out a low whistle. "He did all this with a hockey stick?"

Ari nods. "By the end it was only half a stick, but yes."

That's a lot of anger and violence. "I'll call Erik and tell him we want a meeting with..." I glance at the top of the page. "Felix Ansas. Can I leave it to you to put together our questions for him?"

"I've got it. The rest of them are fine, which surprised me. The club has a reputation for recruiting big guys only, bruisers, so I was sure there would be a lot of problems, but most of the players are settled family men. The most aggressive one is Ansas, and he's the opposite of a bruiser."

"Sound like our talk with him is going to be interesting."

I STARE up at the sign identifying the building in front of me as an animal shelter. "Dáithí?"

"Yes?" He tugs on my arm. "Come on, don't just stand there."

Letting him draw me toward the door, I ask, "Why are we here? I thought you didn't want to have another pet."

He stops. "It's not that I didn't want to—"

"You weren't ready," I correct. I remember when his last pet, Embla, died, and how heartbroken he was. Since then, he's mentioned not wanting another pet when he can't give them security and safety.

It's nice that he now feels like he can.

"So we're here to find you a new baby?" I perk up at the thought that he wanted me here for this personal and important—

"No, I found her. We're here to pick her up," he says, and I try not to deflate too visibly. He asked me to help bring her home—that has to mean something.

I smile and hold the door for him. "I can't wait to meet her."

Inside, we're greeted by a cheerful young woman who recognizes Dáithí. "She's all ready for you!" she announces. "Did you bring a carrier for the car trip?"

Dáithí shakes his head, reaching into his pocket and producing a collar and leash. "We're walking home, so I thought I'd carry her."

Momentary doubt crosses the woman's face. "You're not going to drive?" she checks. "Because if there's an accident and—"

"We're definitely not driving," I assure her. "That's why Dáithí brought me—to make sure nobody bumps into him while he's carrying her. I'm Eoin, by the way."

"I'm Sandra." She bites her lip. "Do you live close by?" I can tell she's still unsure about the whole walking thing but doesn't want to accuse us of lying.

"Dáithí's place is about fifteen minutes from here—off Sturt Street."

She relaxes, her smile returning. "It's such a nice night for a walk too. Okay, I'll go get her while you read through and sign these forms, and then you'll be all set." She pushes a clipboard across the counter, then disappears through a door.

Dáithí picks up a pen and starts skimming the form. "You're going to carry her, hm?" I ask. "So a small pet."

He nods absently, initialing a paragraph.

"But not something like a lizard, that needs an aquarium."

That wins me a glance. "Nope. But we will be stopping at a pet store for me to buy some supplies."

Ah, that explains why he wants me and my portal ability here.

He scrawls his signature at the bottom of the last form, then pushes the clipboard away just as Sandra emerges through the doorway, her arms full of something fluffy.

I blink. "Is that a rabbit?" Of all the animals I was considering, this was not one of them.

Dáithí eagerly holds out his arms and takes her, cuddling her close. "Her name is Elsking."

The happy glow as he bends his face to press against her

furry little head is all I need. It's my life's mission to see that glow on his face every day.

CHAPTER SIXTEEN

Dáithí

Staring into my closet, I try to work out what exactly Eoin has in mind and which outfit would work best for it. Unfortunately, I can't get his instruction of "dress nice" to line up with the fact that we're going to a baseball game.

It's confusing.

When he told me two days ago that the first of the dates he'd planned included the ball game this afternoon, it was both a relief and a tiny disappointment. I do like baseball—as much as I like any sport—and I especially like getting outside in the fresh air and sunshine to perv on physically fit young men in tight pants. There's no downside there. Eoin's picked something that he knows we'll both enjoy, which is the point of all this, isn't it? I guess I just thought...

Honestly, I don't know what I thought. This is a good, solid start.

But it still leaves me with the dilemma of what to wear. Jeans—or shorts, if it's hot enough—and a tee are my usual choices in situations like this, but Eoin said I'd regret it if I wore that.

Turning around, I ask Elsking, who's exploring my bed, "It

has to be jeans, right? Even if he's planning to go somewhere fancy for dinner after, he can't expect me to wear dress pants to a ball game."

She grunts and burrows her head under my pillow, and I smile. I've only had her two days, but already it feels like she's always been here. I was right to adopt again—it's been too long.

"Chinos, maybe?" I muse. "But that still feels pretentious."

Her hindquarters quiver, and I resist the temptation to go over and stroke her. I already spent half the morning loving on her, and it won't be fair to either of us if I start again when I have to leave in...

I glance at my watch. Twenty minutes. Fuck.

"Jeans," I tell her decisively. "But nice ones. And a going-out shirt. If it's still not nice enough for dinner, I can come home and change first." I grab my best jeans, the ones I wear to casual work functions. There are no strategically placed rips or studs, but they are indecently tight. It's not in me to own a pair of jeans that don't show off my assets.

I have a pair of rhinestone-studded Converse that manage to walk the line of being both casual and dressy, which just leaves the shirt...

When Eoin said "nice," did he mean "meeting the boss" nice or "exclusive gay nightclub" nice? Because those are very different things.

In the end I settle on a slim-fitting button-up shirt with a boldly colored repeating pattern of tiny peacocks. The buttons are blue rhinestones, and I leave them half undone to show the tight blue tee underneath, and roll my sleeves halfway to my elbows. It's not supposed to be too warm today, so hopefully I'll be okay.

"Dáithí?" Eoin calls. "Nearly ready?"

I didn't even hear him come in. "Yeah. Do I need a hat?" I hope not. My hair looks great today.

He hesitates. "Bring one."

Blech. Luckily, I have a really cute blinged-out ball cap that goes with these shoes. I grab it, then carefully lift Elsking from where she's snoozing halfway under my pillow.

Out in the living room, Eoin turns away from snooping through my mail, his smile fading into something hot. "You look great."

I twirl—gently, because I don't want to startle my bunny. "Oh yeah? How great?" My eyes narrow as I take him in. "And why did I have to dress nice, but you're wearing jeans and a jersey?"

He comes to take Elsking from me. "Because I don't care what people think of what I wear, but you do."

I'm still puzzling through what that could possibly mean in the context of a baseball game when he gently lays her in her hutch, giving her a few soft pets before he latches it closed. So far, he's been amazing about me having spontaneously added a pet to the equation. It's only been a couple of days, but he hasn't complained even once about us staying here instead of at his place, or about the fact that I didn't want to go out last night in case she got lonely. And at the pet store the other night, he was the one who spent twenty minutes comparing the hutches they had and talking to the salesman about which one would be best for her.

None of that means he wants to stay with me forever, but it does show how much he cares.

By the time we get to the stadium, the whole area is packed. "Where are our seats?" I ask, heading for the entrance. To my surprise, he grabs my hand and leads me around the outside of the stadium. "Where are we going?"

The answer to that is a door marked "Suites and Corporate." My brows shoot up as Eoin hands over two passes for the staff member to scan.

"Thank you so much," she says. "If you head inside and up the escalator to the left, someone will be able to give you directions from there. Enjoy the game."

"We definitely will," Eoin tells her while I mentally try to catch up.

As soon as we're inside, I demand, "Did you get us VIP seats or something?" That's so sweet, but really unnecessary. I can watch the game from—

"Sort of. We're in one of the luxury suites with a bunch of rich people who like to boast about their lives."

I freeze with one foot on the escalator, trip, and would have face-planted if not for Eoin catching me. "Whoa, are you okay?"

Meeting his gaze, I ask slowly, "Are you saying I get to watch tight asses in snug pants while listening to people gossip?"

He grins. "There's food, too."

The sound that escapes my throat might be a squeal, and I throw my arms around his neck and give him a squeeze. "Best— Oof!"

The escalator fucks with me again, and this time I stagger a few feet before regaining my balance. Turning to glare at it, I say, "Note to self: Do not ever get distracted around one of those things."

Eoin's trying not to laugh, but I wouldn't care if he did. I lean up to kiss him. "You're an amazing date planner."

Pink washes into his cheeks. "I'd do anything for you. Let's just hope it goes the way I planned it."

A few minutes later, the suite steward is pointing out where everything is, and I honestly don't think this could go wrong. There's a man passing around canapes on a tray, for one thing, and a self-serve bar set up on a counter. Those are already big wins. There are a couple of sofas and chairs, but the far end of the suite opens into the stadium and has three rows of seats in a box with a fantastic view of the field. We're only a little to the left of home plate.

"...he said they were *old friends*, can you believe that? As if anyone staying at an old friend's home just wanders around naked if there's nothing going on."

My ears perk up, and I follow the sound of the words to a group of three people clustered a few feet away. Two are women, but it's the man who was speaking. All of them are dressed to impress, baseball-game-style. I love it.

"Eoin?" a voice says, and I drag my attention back. "And this must be Dáithí." The man who's come to speak to us is tall, with dark hair that's beginning to go silver and an air of authority. He's wearing chinos and a dress shirt, but somehow manages to seem like he's wearing a suit.

"Yes. It's good to meet you, Dr. Rafter," Eoin says, extending his hand to shake.

"Please call me Vin. I was so pleased when Dr. Griffiths—Rhys—said someone at the DEA wanted to join us today. We're all very excited about his research and the partnership we've built with you."

Ohhhhh. My heart melts just a little. Eoin's thrown himself under a political bus to get me this experience.

"Rhys's work is groundbreaking," he agrees. "My king is always looking for ways to better the lives of his people."

Dr. Rafter—Vin—seizes on that opening. "He might be interested in the work Dr. Leighton is doing. Come and meet her."

Tossing me a wink, Eoin lets himself be drawn away. Once I've helped myself to a drink, I wander over to hover near the gossiping trio, hoping it's not too late to hear more about the naked old friend.

"...she's talking about getting Botox like she's human. Um,

hello? Doesn't she realize she doesn't have human metabolism?" The woman speaking, who I'm pretty sure is a succubus, rolls her eyes and lifts her drink to her lips. When she lowers it again, her gaze falls on me. "Hello. I love that shirt."

Her friends turn to see who she's talking to, and I smile as I step forward to join them. "Thank you. I'm Dáithí, and please don't think I'm rude, but I'm dying to know what happened with the naked old friend."

There's a split-second pause while their brains recalibrate, and then they break into giggles. "Oh, darling, we don't think you're rude at all."

It's halfway through the first inning, and my new friends and I have moved outside to the box seats before Eoin finally breaks free and comes to find me. I startle and nearly spill my drink when he slides into the seat beside me.

"Sorry," he murmurs. "I didn't mean to scare you. All good?"

I lean over to kiss him, buoyed by my enjoyment of the day, how absolutely delicious he is, and the fact that I'm on my third drink. The stadium might only provide human alcohol, but Faith, one of my new besties, brought a flask of some kind of spirits that her cousin's company makes, and it's definitely not human-grade. "All great," I assure him. "This is the best date I've ever been on—or it would be, if you stayed here with me."

The utter joy in his smile warms me from the inside out. "That's the plan. I didn't mean for us to be separated this long." He glances at my glass. "Can I get you another drink? Or something to eat? The steward said he can get us hot dogs, if we want."

"Hot dogs?" I feel myself light up. "Yes. That was the one thing missing. I'll have two with everything and another one of these." I hold my glass out to him. "I think it was the blue bottle and the one with the pink label."

He takes it with a wry look. "How about a beer instead? That tastes better with hot dogs."

He's so right. "Perfect." I grab the front of his jersey and pull him in for another kiss. "Mm. You taste best of all."

"Excuse me, Dáithí's honey of love? Hi. I'm Pamela."

We both turn our heads to see my new friend Pammie tiddling her fingers at Eoin in a wave. "Is the hot dog offer open to the rest of us?"

Eoin grins. "Hi, Pamela. I'm Eoin, and yes. I'm happy to pass your order along."

They all gush their thanks, and once he has everyone's order, he winks at me and stands. "I'll be back in a minute."

As much as I respect Eoin, I have to admit to objectifying him *hard* in that moment, because his ass in those jeans as he walks away is a work of art. It's so unfair—they're not even special going-out jeans or anything, just his everyday ones.

"Mm-hm, Dáithí. You sure got lucky with him," Ned says, not even bothering to keep his voice down. Eoin's chuckle floats back to us as he reenters the suite.

"He's pretty amazing." I can't hide the wistful note in my voice, and they all pounce on it immediately.

"Why does that make you sad?" Faith demands, lowering her sunglasses to peer at me over the top of them. The actual diamonds studded into the frames wink in the sunlight.

I shake my head. "I'm not sad. Eoin's incredible and I'm pretty sure I'd be in love with him if I could let myself. But I don't want to get hurt, so I'm taking it slow." I barely know these people, tipsy or not, so that's the most I'm willing to share with them.

Ned scoffs. "Sweetie, just dive in and worry about getting

hurt if it actually happens. Our lives might be longer than human ones, but that's no reason to second-guess everything."

Pammie makes an agreeing sound. "Holding back from a man that hot who looks at you the way he does just because you might get hurt later is stupid. If he crooked his finger at me, I'd be all in, fuck the consequences." She glances over her shoulder toward the suite. "Don't tell my husband that."

We break out into giggles, and I force myself to take their feedback on board. I'm putting Eoin through this because I've been hurt before, but I'm still here, aren't I? It would devastate me if Eoin walked away... but losing time I *could* spend with him would be just as bad, though in a different way.

The question is, which would be worse?

CHAPTER SEVENTEEN

Eoin

THE OFFICIAL VERDICT isn't in yet, but based on the way Dáithí's smiling and clinging to my side, I'd say our date was a success. Since the moment I sat down and handed him his beer, with the promise that the hot dogs were on their way, he's been affectionate and happy. At first I thought that was because of the flask Faith kept passing around, but he's not showing signs of being drunk, and it's been long enough since he had any of that for it to have worn off anyway.

No, this is genuinely happy Dáithí.

"Got your keys?" I ask as we approach his front door. He has his head bent over his phone, texting with one hand. His new friends invited him to their group chat so they could keep him up to date with... I'm not sure, exactly. Something about a husband's naked friend? And I think Botox was mentioned as well, which confused me, since Dáithí won't ever need it. We're *elves*, after all. Self-healing wrinkles is simple, if we even allow ourselves to age to the point of getting them.

"Hm?" he asks, absorbed in whatever he's reading. He

only parted from them forty minutes ago, but the gossip must be piling up.

"Keys, love. We need to go inside. Unless you'd like to go sit in the park?" It's a beautiful evening, and I wouldn't mind some more outdoor time.

"In my pocket. Wait, huh?" He looks up. "What did you say?"

"We need your keys to get inside, or we can go to the park if you'd rather," I repeat. He doesn't often let down his guard enough for me to see this distracted side of him, and I love it. Regular Dáithí is sassy and sexy and sharp, but private Dáithí is all that plus sensitive and soft and adorable.

"Oh, let's go to the park. It's been such a gorgeous day, but I'd love to actually sit in the grass."

"Me, too." I turn away from his door in the direc—

"Where are you going?" His firm tug on the arm that's wound through mine stops me before he speaks.

"Park?" I point east. Most of us elves who live in cities either try to find homes with yards and gardens or green spaces nearby. Dáithí's no exception—there's a small but really lovely park only half a block from here.

He shakes his head. "I need to change first, Eoin. I'll split a seam if I try to sit on the ground in these jeans, and the last thing this shirt needs is grass stains. Anyway, I want to bring Elsking with us. She hasn't had park time since she came to live with me."

"Okay." I nod. "So... keys?" My restraint in not mentioning that we're back where we started is medal-worthy.

"It's in my left front pocket," Dáithí says with the kind of heavy patience that implies I should have known that.

We stare at each other, neither of us moving.

"Um... are you going to get it out?"

He sighs. "Both my hands are busy. Could you get it, please?"

I don't bother trying to hold back my laugh. Cheeky little shit. He's got his phone in one hand and the other is holding my arm—it's not like he needs them to perform surgery. "Of course. Always happy to put my hand in your pocket, love. Especially when your jeans are so very tight."

He blows me a kiss, and I take my time feeling around for the key. It's not like he could have fit anything else in that pocket, so it's easy to find, but we both enjoy having me draw it out.

When we finally get inside, he beelines over to Elsking's hutch to pet and coo at her while he checks her water bowl. "Just give me five minutes to change and grab your leash," he promises her, "and we'll go out. You'll like it." He glances my way as he heads toward the bedroom. "Do you want to grab a couple of water bottles and some fruit?"

"I got it," I assure him. I'm familiar enough with his kitchen to bag up a small picnic of snacks for us, and then I call, "Is it okay if I take Elsking out of the hutch for cuddles?" She's been alone most of the day, and even though Dáithí said rabbits are okay with that, I don't think she should have to wait any longer for social time.

"Sure!"

Elsking is more than happy to leave her hutch, and with her cuddled in my arms—she truly is so affectionate—I wander back into the kitchen. I obviously didn't clean his apartment this morning, since I wasn't about to pass up the ball game, but next weekend might work out, and I want to get an idea of what I'll be tackling. Obviously I would never reorganize his space without his approval, but I've noticed that he doesn't have much of a system for pantry goods, and there are multiples of some items.

"You can help yourself if you're hungry," he says from behind me. "You know that, right?"

I turn and smile at him, taking in how good he looks in faded, worn-out jeans and an equally old chest-hugging T-shirt, Elsking's purple leash trailing from his hand. My Dáithí would be beautiful in anything. "Thank you, I know, but I'm not hungry," I assure him. "I was just wondering if you'd like me to install a spice rack on the inside of the cabinet door."

He cocks his head. "Say again?"

I gesture into the cabinet. "See how everything's all stacked up randomly, making it hard to find things? That's how you've ended up with four unopened jars of ground cinnamon, right?"

"Right." He pulls a face. "It never seems to be there when I want it, but as soon as I buy a new one, I find it." He pauses. "Wait, did you say *four*?"

I nod. "Yep. But if you want, I can install a spice rack on the inside of the door, so you'll be able to see it right away, no need to rummage through everything else at all. And it will free up more room too."

He stares at me. "That would be great, but... do you really want to waste time doing that?"

Huffing, I give him a wry look. "It's not a waste if it makes things easier for you. I can take care of it when I clean your place. Is there anything else you want done, or that bugs you?"

Slowly, he shakes his head, the softness in his gaze telling me I'm winning points. "Let me think about it and get back to you. There are better things we can be doing right now than talking about cabinets." He comes forward and fastens Elsking's leash to her collar, then takes her from me, bending to croon about how lucky she is that he's not the jealous type. Grinning, I grab the bag of snacks and follow them outside.

It doesn't take long for us to get to the park, and at this

time on a Saturday evening, it's deserted. The kids who use the playground equipment have gone home, and it's too early for the older teens who use it as a make-out and hangout spot. They like to wait for full darkness.

We settle on a grassy spot that's still faintly warm from the day's sun. Dáithí and I lie back and kick off our shoes and socks, and Elsking explores the area within the reach of her leash, periodically returning to nibble at our fingers. Above us, the sky is slowly darkening from the brilliant cerulean of the day through shades of indigo. Only the brightest stars are visible just yet—though, I think that might actually be a planet. I don't know enough about this dimension to be sure.

"I should learn about the astronomy here," I muse. "I keep meaning to, but there always seems to be something else to do."

Dáithí's hand brushes mine, and then he twines our fingers together. "Same. The stars are pretty, though. I missed seeing the night sky when the anomalies got bad." He pauses. "It's different here, but I think it's better that way."

"Mm." I know what he means. If the night sky was the same as it had been back home, it would have just made the fact that we lost everything else more painful. I tighten my fingers in his.

He seems to understand, squeezing back. "Thank you for today," he murmurs. "It was perfect."

Warmth spreads through my chest. "I'm glad."

We lie there for a while, thinking our own thoughts but somehow keeping each other company, and just when I'm beginning to feel hungry, Dáithí sits up and grabs the snack bag. He coos at Elsking and offers her something—probably the lettuce I put in for her—then leans over me with a bunch of grapes in his hand.

"Open," he says quietly, and I open my mouth and let him feed me grapes, one at a time. He alternates between giving them to me and eating them himself, propped on an elbow beside me, and I keep my eyes on his face. The faint smile as he takes care of us both feeds my soul.

Eventually, the grapes are gone, and Dáithí sits up again. I'm half expecting him to offer me water next, but instead I feel his hands at my waist and then the night air on my cock as he frees it.

"Dáithí—"

"Shh. I'm still hungry, Eoin."

I huff and prop myself up on my elbows so I can see him bent over my rapidly hardening dick, which doesn't care about the law or modesty. "We're in a public place."

His hair falls into his eyes as he glances at me. "It's dark, and nobody's here. Trust me."

Our gazes hold for another few seconds, and then I lie back down in tacit assent, waiting for whatever he does next.

Which is to lick the head of my dick. "Mmm," he murmurs. "You taste better than grapes ever could." He sets to work tormenting me. There's no other way to describe the way he licks and lightly nibbles when I want—when he *knows* I want—a firm touch. He does this sometimes, edging me until I can't remember my own name. I wish I could say I hated it.

With my pants still on, he doesn't have a lot of room to work, but he's wrapped his hand around the base of my cock, and it grounds me as his lips and tongue lavish attention on the rest, the butterfly touches and phantom kisses merging with the cooling evening air and the darkness that envelops us to send me into a hazy, sensation-filled dream state. I stare up at the icy pinpricks that are the stars as little shocks of pleasure race through my body, my muscles slowly becoming tighter as my breathing begins to race and hitch.

And then Dáithí's hot mouth swallows me and my vision whites out.

CHAPTER EIGHTEEN

Dáithí

I'M NOT surprised to look up and see all four members of Team Bro gathered around my desk midafternoon on Monday. What does surprise me is that it took them this long to make an appearance.

"Oh, yay. Just who I wanted taking up my space."

"You're so mean," Hagen says, but it's not a complaint. "No wonder Eoin's crazy about you."

I refuse to encourage him by smiling. "Did you need something? Because last time I checked, we all *work* here." If any of them tries to suggest—

"Since Brandt and the king are involved, the Summit of Love counts as work," Alistair declares. My spray bottle is in my hand without conscious effort, and I'm spritzing water at him before he finishes speaking. "Hey!"

"Your brand of ridiculous is not going to become part of my workday. And I told you to stop calling it that!"

"But—" Caolan's hand over his mouth stops him from saying anything else, and Hagen goes to the utility closet without being asked to get the mop. Alistair looks at it like he's never seen one before. I didn't spritz him that hard, so there shouldn't be more than a few droplets on the floor.

"Is this what DEA reception is like all the time?" Andrew asks. "I love Candice, but she's never this entertaining."

I point the bottle in his direction, and he puts his hands up to ward me off.

"No, please. I apologize. This shirt is silk. The water..." He shudders, as though even thinking about it is painful. I'm not sure if he's joking or not.

"Why are you wearing a silk shirt to work?" Caolan asks as Alistair takes the mop and gives the floor a few cursory swabs. "David says work clothes should be practical." His adoration of his boyfriend shines through the simple sentence. It's sweet... and also weird. David Carew is admirable, I don't mind admitting that, and he's definitely a hottie, but I don't think he's worthy of worship. Is that a side effect of love? If Eoin and I stay together, will I one day consider him to be the ultimate authority on everything, including shirt fabrics?

"David wears polyester blend shirts," Andrew replies with a sniff. "I don't know where I went wrong with him."

There's clearly some very complex history here that only makes sense to the Earth species, and honestly, both Andrew and David have boring taste in shirts, whatever they're made of, so I'm going to move this conversation along.

"Well, if there's nothing you need from me—"

"We do!" Alistair cries. "We need an update. The first date was on the weekend, wasn't it? The panel needs details in order to offer feedback, and we're the designated representatives of the panel." He waves a hand to encompass the four of them.

I'm never getting control of this situation back. Note to self: Be careful when asking for help; it might not end up being what you had in mind.

"What do you need to know?" It's the fastest way to get rid of them.

They exchange glances. "You were going to a baseball game, right? You said you like baseball," Hagen prompts.

I narrow my eyes. "You knew it wasn't just the game, didn't you?"

They look guilty. "Maybe."

"Why didn't you tell me? Do you know how close I came to not being appropriately dressed?" I plant my hands on my hips.

Alistair frowns. "But you knew it was a ball game. How could you be inappropriately dressed for a ball game? Jeans, T-shirt, maybe a hoodie and ballcap. Done."

Sighing, Andrew shakes his head and says to me, "I'm sorry about him. He thinks clothes are to keep you warm—unless it's a costume."

"Huh?" The overgrown hellhound still looks confused, so I take pity on him.

"It was a luxury suite, Alistair. Some of the other guests were wearing *diamonds*." Some were in jeans and tees, too, but that's not the point. *I* would have felt underdressed in that.

"Oh. That sounds like a good way to make a ball game less fun."

They all look at me expectantly, waiting to see if I agree.

I shake my head. "It was the best," I inform them. "All the benefits of baseball with the added fun of free-flowing cocktails, food, and gossip. He showed how well he knows me."

"So your clothes were okay after all?" Caolan asks.

My smile is involuntary. "Yes. Eoin told me to dress nice without ruining the surprise."

"He gets points for that," Hagen murmurs, "and for planning a date that suits your interests."

The ball of hope that I'm no longer able to push down compels me to add, "After, we took Elsking to the park and lay in the grass under the stars." They don't need to know what else we did under the stars, but Eoin deserves extra points for ending our date on the perfect note.

"Aww," Caolan says. "That's so romantic. You don't have a yard, do you?"

I shake my head. "No." He and Hagen will understand how valuable time spent just lying in the grass is for me—for any elf.

"Wait." Andrew holds up a finger. "Who's Elsking? Do you have a child? Nobody told me that."

"He got a pet rabbit last week, remember?" Alistair looks at me. "Elsking is the rabbit, right? There isn't another person involved that we should know about?"

And just like that, any tolerance I was feeling flees. "Elsking is my new pet," I confirm flatly.

"Why a rabbit?" Hagen asks. "They don't do very much."

Scoffing, Andrew says, "A rabbit is an excellent choice. Don't you know how good their fur is for fiber arts?" He turns to me expectantly. "Angora, yes? What type? English produces more hair, but the fur from a Satin Angora has a much nicer finish."

I stare at him, but thankfully, I'm not the only one. "What are you talking about?" Caolan demands. "Angwhat?"

"Fiber arts?" Alistair says. "Do you mean knitting? That's sheep fur, Andrew." He frowns. "Wait. Sheep... hair? Wool! Sheep wool."

Andrew rolls his eyes. "There are many animals that produce fibers that are good for weaving and knitting," he informs us. "Rabbits included."

That's something I didn't know. Did he say angora? I have a sweater made of that—it's super soft. I just didn't know it was rabbit fur. "They don't hurt the bunnies to get their hair, do they?"

"No. I believe rabbits shed fur naturally and only need to be brushed to collect it."

The relief is almost dizzying. I couldn't force Elsking to live in the same house as something that caused harm to one of her kind, but I *really* didn't want to get rid of that sweater. It fits perfectly and looks great on me.

"Elsking isn't that kind of rabbit," I say firmly, though I don't actually know that for sure. Sandra at the shelter would have said if she was, wouldn't she? There was mention of regular brushing, but not anything about knitting with her fur. I make a mental note to check on that.

Not that I know how to knit or have any interest in learning.

"What kind—"

"We're getting off topic," Hagen interrupts, shooting Caolan an apologetic look. "The rabbit's fur isn't important. How's Eoin with her?"

I shrug. "Good." The memory of him taking her out of the hutch and giving her cuddles without me asking brings a smile to my face. "It's only been a few days, but he's good with her."

"No resentment?"

"No." How could Eoin resent a precious bunny? She's the sweetest. And even if she wasn't, he's always been good with animals.

"It might be too soon for that to show," Alistair muses, and I reach the end of my patience.

"You've got the information you came for. Go report back to the others so you can all give me your expert feedback." I make sure to sound as sarcastic as possible.

"Before we go, we need to talk about Eoin working on reception," Caolan says, pulling out his phone and tapping the screen. "Ari checked his schedule, and the first possible option is a week from Thursday. He only has two meetings that day, and Ari says they can both be rescheduled. Otherwise it will need to be next month."

"Are you asking my permission?" That would be a first.

Hagen laughs. "No, of course not. We're letting you know as a courtesy so you'll have time to make a list of anything essential he needs to know about the DEA specifically. Alistair talked to Candice, and she has a training manual that she's used to teach people the job in the past, so it's just the personal stuff you need to worry about."

"Plus she said he can call her if he has problems," Alistair adds helpfully.

I bite my lip. "That might not be a good idea. What if he struggles? Candice can't do her job *and* mine. Maybe he should call me if he has problems. I can hang out in the conference room for the day." My streaming apps work from anywhere.

The way all four of them forcefully disagree makes me lean back.

"You won't be here that day," Caolan says, "and we've told Candice to get one of the temps who cover when she has time off to come in that day. No matter what happens, both receptions will be taken care of."

It's a little worrying that I'm so easy to replace. "Who's paying for that?"

"It's coming out of the executive cost center," Hagen assures me. "Brandt okayed it."

"Does his majesty know?"

"Brandt okayed it. I didn't ask any questions after that."

That gets a laugh from me, but I decide to let it go. Eoin's going to ask the same thing, and he'll definitely follow up with the king to make sure he approves. The last thing either of us wants is to get fired for misappropriation of government funds.

"Fine. Thursday next week. I'll make sure I have a cheat

sheet for him before then. What am I supposed to do that day?"

"Sleep in," Hagen suggests.

"Go for a hike," Caolan adds.

"Play with your rabbit." Alistair frowns. "That sounds dirty, somehow."

For the love of... "You are never allowed near Elsking."

"Just enjoy the time off," Andrew cuts in before Alistair can argue. "It's a gift from Eoin—another way he's trying to show you how earnest he is about this."

He's right. "Yeah. Good point. Thank you. For... everything." I actually mean it.

Andrew's fangs peek out as he grins. "An excellent way to show thanks is with cake."

"There's some in the break room," I tell him, and revulsion flashes across his face.

"Twinkies are not—"

"I don't want to be part of this argument again." It's Alistair's turn to cut in. He leans on the raised part of my desk and meets my gaze. "How do you think it's going so far?"

I blink. "You mean... the challenges?"

He nods.

"Well... good, I guess. There's only been one date, so it might be too soon to tell."

He makes an odd sort of face, his eyebrows bouncing around. "But do you feel good about it? Like Eoin's going to stick it out?"

The words catch in my throat, because while hope is now a permanent part of my being, saying things out loud might jinx them. "He hasn't backed out yet." It's a compromise.

Alistair seems disappointed by my lack of commitment. "Does that make you happy?"

Yes. Again, the word sticks, but it must show on my face, because they all break out in smiles.

CHAPTER NINETEEN

Eoin

A THICK FOLDER drops onto my desk, breaking my concentration. I glance at it, then up at Niamh, who's now shamelessly looking at my screen. "What are you doing? Does that say 'custom leather collars'? I didn't need to know this about you, boss."

Around us, heads pop up. Everyone on my team has sharp hearing and the ability to multitask, and their experience in the army means their situational awareness is second-to-none. It's why I try not to have personal or classified conversations in here.

"Collars?" Brayan says. "Is Eoin watching porn? How did you get around the firewall?"

It's not just me who turns to stare at him, and his face goes red as he hurries to add, "Not that I've ever tried to watch porn at work. That would be unprofessional."

"Today seems to be the day for learning unwanted information about my colleagues' sexual interests," Niamh says. "Could I get trauma leave for this? I feel like I need a day off to process what I've learned and bleach my brain."

"Nobody's getting trauma leave, and nobody's watching

porn at work," I declare, exasperated. I scroll back up to the top of the webpage. "This site is for custom pet collars. Do we need to have a training session about the need to gather information before making conclusions?"

"It's not like I used a combat spell," she protests. "What—"

"Did you need something?"

There's an instant of hesitation while she calculates whether she can push her luck, but I've got my resting boss face firmly in place, so she huffs and taps a finger on the folder. "These are the updated monthly reports from the teams with the viceroys. Most of them are fine, but you should look at the one from the Pacific Islands. It seems like the team leader wants us to read between the lines."

Frowning, I reach for the folder and find the relevant report. "Do I need to alert His Majesty?" Skimming the first paragraph, I immediately see what she means.

"I don't think so. The vibe I got wasn't about security issues, more like the team needs a shakeup."

The more I read, the more I'm inclined to agree. The report doesn't outright state that there are tensions within the team there, but it's not hard to spot the insinuation. "Pull the details of everyone on the roster there and see if you can spot any obvious reasons for conflict," I order. "I'll follow up with you about it tomorrow, and we'll go from there." The next step would be a call with the team lead in question, but I want to have the relevant background fresh in my mind before then.

"On it," Niamh assures me, hesitates again as her gaze goes to my screen, then turns and heads back to her desk.

I flip quickly through the rest of the reports, since I have them in my hands, but she's right that everything looks fine. I'll do a thorough read prior to my monthly calls with the team leaders next week, but it's pretty much all routine.

There's no big threat to the viceroys here on Earth, just like there isn't one to the king.

A chat box pops up on my screen just as I turn my attention back to the custom pet accessories site.

> The hockey people are here for your eleven o'clock meeting. Erik brought three people with him.

Shit, is it that time already? I glance at the clock in the bottom corner of the screen, and yes, I'm behind on my work for the morning. "Ari, meeting," I say while I type my reply.

> Thanks—on our way. Impressions of the new people?

Ari stops beside my desk, his tablet in hand, and we both wait for Dáithí's answer.

> One polite professional, one arrogant asshole, and one who needs therapy.

"That's an interesting take," Ari murmurs. "I wonder who's who?"

I click the message to like it, then lock my computer and stand. "Let's go find out." For all our sakes, I hope this meeting goes well and resolves our concerns. Raðulfr and Jared both want the collaboration with the Warhammers to go ahead, and the PR department has added their vote as well. Not to mention, if I have to veto this, I'll probably need to have a conversation with an angry Jared. That's not going to go well for me.

Ari waits until we're in the hallway before saying casually, "So... pet collars."

"Do we have to do this? We're working." My attempt to sound professional is thwarted by the plaintive note in my voice.

"I'm just saying, you don't have a pet. Which means—"

"Dáithí didn't have many options to choose from when he got Elsking's collar, and I know he wasn't thrilled with what he picked," I explain, hoping to just get it over with. "It's not a crime for me to look at getting one for her that he'd like better."

"That's cool. Did you see anything that would work?"

I shoot him a sideways glance, but it doesn't seem like he's teasing. "Maybe. I need to email the company and see if they have the options I want."

He nods, and as we come out into reception, lowers his voice and adds, "You should check with Dáithí and see if he has preferences too."

I roll my eyes at him. "I'm not going to order anything without checking first." I give Dáithí a smile and a wave, loving the way his face lights up as he smiles back, and then we turn toward our waiting visitors.

It only takes one glance to know which is the polite professional—he's rising from his seat, a smile on his face.

"Hi, Eoin, Ari," Erik says, stepping forward to shake hands. "It's good to see you again." There's a slightly harried undertone to the words, which concerns me. Is he not confident in Ansas's explanation?

"Thanks for coming in," I reply. "I know you were hoping to be further along with plans by now."

"It's no problem," he assures me, then half turns to gesture to the polite professional. "This is Craig Voss, our general manager. Craig, Eoin Feirstrigh and Ari Oensjord."

"Great to meet you both," Craig says. "We appreciate you giving Felix the opportunity to clarify the situation."

I open my mouth, but my reply is cut off by a very loud snort. "Like there's any clarification that could make Ansas palatable."

Craig's smile disappears, and Erik's face falls. "Now,

Coach, maybe let these guys get to know your sense of humor before you start with the jokes."

Ah. His stress is suddenly completely understandable. And I'm pretty sure I know who the arrogant asshole is.

"Jokes? Who—"

"This is Coach Franks," Erik cuts in desperately.

I nod, but don't offer to shake hands. "Coach." My gaze slides to the last member of the group, who Dáithí believes is in need of therapy. Based on his background check, I suspect it would be for anger management. "And you're Felix Ansas."

He nods and comes forward, hand half outstretched as if he's not sure I'll take it. "Thank you for this meeting." He's pale and his jaw is tight. I'm sure he's been lectured on how important this is for the team.

I shake his hand, and some of his tension eases. He offers it to Ari too.

Ari hesitates.

Even as I glance at him in surprise, mortification flashes across Ansas's face and he drops his arm.

"Let's take this to the conference room," I suggest, eager to distract from the awkward moment. "Down this hallway, gentlemen."

As we find places around the big table, I give Ari a "what the fuck?" look, and he pulls a slight face in return. Whatever it was, he regrets it.

"We won't take up more of your time than we have to," I say, then nod to Ari, who casts the photos from the enforcement report onto the big screen at the front of the room.

"Our concerns stem from this incident, which led to charges of aggravated assault and destruction of property," he says calmly. "Mr. Ansas, could you cast some light on what happened?"

Erik jumps in. "The assault charge was dismissed."

"We're aware, and we're in no way implying it shouldn't

have been, but we want to understand why Mr. Ansas was even in a position for the charge to be laid."

Felix clears his throat. "I regret everything that happened that night. Tony and I had an argument earlier that day, and I'd been wallowing over it... It was poor decision-making on my part. I've never done anything like that before or since."

I study his face. This was the only reported incident of violence Ari found, but "we argued and I was mad" is a lack-luster reason for the level of damage that was caused. The kind of rage needed for this is usually caused by one of two things: a deeply triggering event, or a propensity for violence.

It's the latter that we're worried about.

"We know that this was an isolated incident," Ari agrees, "but you do have a reputation for being short-tempered on the ice also. We're concerned by your inability to control your anger."

Not the most diplomatic way to have phrased it. Ari's really not on his game today, and I make a mental note to follow up with him. He seemed fine before.

"I'm *paid* to be aggressive on the ice," Felix answers with a hint of heat. "Aside from that one time, I've never been phys-ical off it."

Ari raises a brow. "You're paid to assault your own teammates?"

"Getting back to what happened that night," I cut in, stomping my foot down on Ari's. What the fuck is wrong with him? "You mentioned that you'd been 'wallowing.' Do you mean that there was alcohol involved?" Alcohol-fueled crimes are rare in the community, since high metabolism makes it hard to remain drunk for long, even with specialty liquor, but they do still happen.

He shakes his head. The nerves are gone now, and he looks pissed. Probably with Ari. "No, I wasn't drinking. I had a game the next day, and I never drink the night before a game. I was just so mad." His gaze drops to the tabletop.

"I'm sorry, we need to know why. We need to be sure it's not something likely to come up when you're in the company of the king."

Felix shakes his head. "It won't." He looks so uncomfortable that I want to take his word for it, but I've never let anything slide when it comes to Raðulfr's safety.

"I'm sure you're right, but we need—"

Coach Franks bangs his hands on the table. "For fuck's sake, it was just homo drama! The gays always make a big deal of shit."

Erik closes his eyes, and Felix's face flushes with angry color, but even as I process the fact that he really did say that, Craig snaps, "That's enough, Coach."

"I'm just clearing shit up so—"

"*Enough.*"

I meet Erik's gaze. "Neither the DEA nor the king personally will agree to be associated with any organization that condones homophobia." I'm surprised I even need to say it. I've been told that homophobia is something humans invented after the species wars, but it's not widespread in the community.

Erik nods and starts to speak, but Craig steps in. "The Warhammers are committed to being inclusive. Homophobia isn't tolerated."

Felix's jaw tenses in a way that tells me his experience hasn't reflected that, and I make a mental note to follow this up before I sign off on anything.

Of course, it might be a moot point if we don't get the violence issue resolved. I look him in the eye. "Would you be more comfortable if we continued this conversation privately?" I need the answers, but that doesn't mean he has to share them with everyone in this room.

He shakes his head. "Thanks for the offer, but it's... fine. Tony and I had been together for a few years, and I found out that day that he'd been seeing other people too. That's what we argued about. I never meant to hurt him, I swear. He jumped between my stick and the window, and I couldn't stop it in time."

I've seen the surveillance footage, including the way Felix immediately threw the broken hockey stick aside and rushed to check his unintended victim was okay, so I believe that. As for the rest... I'm sure there's more to the story, hurtful words to go along with hurtful actions. I don't need to know them.

Raðulfr isn't going to date Felix and then cheat on him, so while I might not ever want a friend of mine to get involved with Felix Ansas, he doesn't pose a danger to my king.

Now all I need to worry about is whatever crisis of intelligence Ari's having. I need him in top form, both here at work and as part of my support team for the Summit of Love.

CHAPTER TWENTY

Dáithí

"You should take Elsking with you," Eoin orders, appearing in my bedroom doorway. "I'm not planning to use any chemicals with harsh smells or anything, but I'll be moving stuff around and the noise might..." He blinks, taking me in fully. "Or if you're going to wear that, I could clean another day and—"

I laugh and saucily blow him a kiss. "I'll still be wearing it when I get home and when we go out tonight. Where are we going, again?" I cock a hip, letting the sexy jockstrap highlight some of my best features. Maybe if he's distracted, he'll let some of the details slip.

"Hmm." His heavy-lidded gaze and the little smile on his face as he looks at me make me feel like a god.

"Eoin? Where are we going tonight?" I plant a hand on my hip, letting my fingers frame the good stuff. "Is this dress code appropriate?"

That snaps him out of his lust-induced haze, and his gaze rises to meet mine, brows drawing together. "Not on its own. People drool over you when you're fully clothed, Dáithí—give my poor jealous brain a tiny break and keep this just for me."

It always gives me a thrill when he says something like that... well, as long as he doesn't phrase it as a demand. I've never liked being bossed around by boyfriends. Of course, before Eoin and I hooked up, I also didn't like displays of jealousy or possessiveness, but somehow, from him, it's... not toxic.

I stroll over to him and loosely drape my arms over his shoulders as his hands lightly grip my hips. "I can do that. You'll be the only one who knows what's under my clothes tonight at... Where are we going, again?" Leaning in, I feather kisses along the side of his neck, and his breath catches.

"Nice try." Firming his hold on my hips, he sets me away from him—but still within arm's reach. The bulge in his pants is proof of how strong his willpower is. "You're good, but I'm not spoiling the surprise."

My eyes shoot back to his face and my heart rate picks up. "The surprise? As in... *the* surprise from the list of challenges?" He said that tonight was one of the planned dates, but maybe he's changed his mind and swapped it with something else? Or he could have decided to combine two of the tasks into one.

"No." He shakes his head, then leans over to drop a kiss on my mouth. "Just a regular surprise. I'm saving *the* surprise for another time."

My adrenaline begins to settle. I'm not sure why the idea of tonight being the surprise task was such a big deal, but my subconscious clearly has feelings about it. To cover that up, I heave a giant sigh and turn to walk back to the bed, putting extra sway into every step. I know what this jockstrap looks like from behind.

The pained sound Eoin makes assures me it was worth every penny of the ridiculously high price tag.

"Well, if you're not going to tell me anything about tonight, I'm going to get dressed and go out. You really won't let me stay?" I pick up my jeans and look over my shoulder as I bend to step into them.

Glazed eyes look back at me, and he gives his head a little shake, as if to clear it. "Would you be able to sit back and not try to help while I clean the place from top to bottom? I'm going to need to move your stuff around to do that, you know."

I open my mouth to say that of course I could, then reconsider. Sitting back and letting other people be in charge isn't something I'm known for. "Okay, fine. I'll go out. Jared said he was home alone this morning, and I can go over there." I zip and button, then reach for my tee.

"Oh. Maybe you shouldn't take Elsking, then." He frowns worriedly as he glances back toward the living room. "Jared has a cat."

"Do cats and rabbits not get along?" I haven't looked up information like that yet, since I only just let myself get one pet. I need more time before I'm ready for a second one.

He shrugs, but the worry doesn't fade. "I don't know, but if they don't, Elsking shouldn't have to suffer because of our ignorance. It might be better if she stayed here. I can move her from room to room to keep the noise from bothering her too much. It's still a disruption, but..." He catches sight of my indulgent smile. "What?"

"Nothing. Just..." I scramble for something to say that's not "you're earning so many points on the tasks you don't know about." "You know I'd never let her get hurt, right?"

"Pft. Of course you wouldn't. But she still might get scared, and she shouldn't have to go through that."

My heart melts. "I'll call Jared and ask him if his cat likes rabbits."

"While you're doing that, I'll check Google," he says, and goes in search of his phone.

Jared answers on the second ring. "Hi. If you're calling to

ask if you can come over, yes, the offer's still open. I went to the farmer's market this morning and got some amazing cheeses and cake, and my garden is flooded with sun."

If I hadn't been planning to go before, I would be now. "That sounds perfect. I have a question, though—Eoin reminded me you have a cat."

"That's not a question, but yes, I do. Her name is Marge. You're not allergic, are you?" Concern filters through the question.

"No, but Eoin thinks his cleaning might be disruptive for Elsking, so I was going to bring her... but I don't know if cats and rabbits are friend or foe."

Jared's chuckle is warm and understanding. "Mostly friend, but it depends on the cat. We're in luck, though, because Margie gets along great with the classroom rabbit when I bring her in with me to do classroom chores. I think they'll be fine, but if it looks like there might be a problem, I can put Marge inside."

"Are you sure?" That doesn't seem fair.

"Yes. She can have garden time whenever she wants. Elsking deserves a turn too. But I really don't think there will be a problem."

"Thank you. In that case, we'll be there in half an hour or so. Can I bring anything? Bread for the cheese, maybe?"

"I've got everything we need," he assures me. "Just one thing, though—my friend Felix called before and is going to stop by."

My gossip radar perks up. "Felix the hockey player?" Eoin wouldn't say much about the meeting the other day, only that he'd given the collaboration a green light. I don't even know what the meeting was about, exactly, that needed one of the players there, looking like he wanted to vomit.

"That's him."

"Great! I can't wait to meet him." And not just because I'm nosy.

"See you soon, then."

I lower my phone as Eoin reappears, staring at his. "This says they usually get along, but sometimes they need time to get to know each other first."

"Jared said his cat's been around rabbits before," I report. "You can stop worrying."

His relieved smile makes me wonder again if I'm setting myself up for heartbreak. There's no question in my mind that I love Eoin more than I ever did Alan, no matter how hard I've tried not to.

FELIX IS ALREADY at Jared's house when I arrive, stretched out on the clover lawn with his eyes closed, sunning himself. It strikes me again that he's smaller than I'd expected, based on what Jared's said about him and the fact that he's a hockey player. Some people have big personalities, even when they're absent.

I set Elsking's travel crate down, and Jared and I watch closely as Marge wanders over to investigate. We agreed that if she seems at all aggressive, we won't even try introducing them properly.

Marge sniffs around the front of the carrier, and Elsking slowly eases forward, her nose twitching. For a moment, they study each other, separated by the steel grill of the door, and then they touch noses.

"I think it's okay," I whisper, not wanting to break the moment of connection. Neither of them seems bothered—no fear, no aggression.

"Yeah." Jared steps forward and scoops Marge away from the crate. "Let her out, and let's see."

Our fears were completely unfounded, and within five minutes, the two animals are curled around each other in a sunny patch of clover, Marge grooming Elsking, whose eyes are half closed as if she's being pampered at a day spa.

"I foresee many playdates in our future," Jared says at last, stepping over them to settle himself beside Felix. "Take a seat, Dáithí, and meet Felix."

I lower myself to the ground and dig my fingers into the clover, the rush of growing energy tingling through me. I love nature. "Hi, again. Felix came into the DEA for a meeting this week," I explain to Jared.

"I know, but he was too nervous to remember anyone he met."

"Except that one asshole," Felix grumbles, and my hackles go up. He better not be talking about Eoin.

"Asshole?" I ask, and the dangerous edge has Felix opening one eye, but he doesn't back down.

"Yeah. He accused me of assaulting people."

That doesn't sound like Eoin, not unless it was true... and I doubt Felix would be so pissed about it if it was.

"Can you describe him?" Jared asks diplomatically. "How many of our people were in that meeting?"

My ire momentarily dips at the completely natural way Jared said "our people." He's taking ownership of us now, just like a consort should.

"Two," I tell him. "Eoin and Ari." Of the two, Eoin's the most likely to be an asshole, but that doesn't mean I'm just going to sit back and let some random felid I don't know say so.

Felix opens his other eye and sits up. "Which was which? The head guy, the one in charge, he was okay. Professional, at least. It was the other guy who was a dick."

Jared and I exchange a startled look. "*Ari* was a dick?" I ask.

"Are you sure?" Jared adds, then shakes his head. "Wow, stupid question. I just mean… Ari was the asshole? Really?"

I want to defend Eoin, but he and Jared had a rocky introduction, and even though they're good now, Jared totally gets a pass on the whole calling-Eoin-an-asshole thing.

"I don't know," Felix says with heavy sarcasm. "Which one is he?"

"Long hair." That's probably the easiest way for him to differentiate between them.

"Then yeah, he was the asshole. Is that not normal for him?"

We both shake our heads.

"Great," he mutters. "Guess I just bring it out in people."

"You said he accused you of assault? Why? You don't have to say," I tack on, even though it hurts to do so. I'm desperately curious.

Felix leans back on his hands. "It's not a secret. I'm sure people at your office are talking about it."

Jared laughs. "If Dáithí doesn't know about it, they're not talking about it. Eoin's his boyfriend."

"He's not—" I start, but he gives me a "be serious" look, and I subside.

Felix glances between us. "That was the other guy? The nicer one?"

"I'd argue that," Jared jokes, "but yes. And yes, he's Dáithí's boyfriend, even if it is complicated right now."

"That sounds like an interesting story." Felix quirks a brow at me, not even trying to be subtle. I like him.

"I'll trade you, your story for mine. Because Eoin's annoyingly strict about confidentiality and won't tell me even if I beg." Which I won't. It sets a bad precedent to beg outside of sex.

"Deal."

CHAPTER TWENTY-ONE

Dáithí

"Like I said, it's not a secret," he continues. "Fifteen years ago, I went to my ex-boyfriend's house with my hockey stick and broke all his windows, beat the crap out of his car, and turned his mailbox into scrap metal. Unfortunately, he came out of the house and got in the way, and I accidentally hit him as well."

Jared's face is horrified. "*Accidentally?*"

"Yeah. He got between the stick and the window beside the door after I'd already started swinging, and I couldn't pull back enough to stop it. It didn't hit him hard, though. He got bruised, but not too badly. The assault charges were dismissed because he had one of those doorbell cameras, and the video proved it wasn't intentional."

That seems to appease Jared a little, but not completely. He's a very nonviolent person, which makes his love of hockey surprising.

I, on the other hand, can totally appreciate the occasional need to smash a window. "What'd he do?"

"My ex?"

I nod, and Felix sighs. "He cheated. A lot. The whole

three years we were together, it turned out. We'd agreed to be monogamous, but I'd found out that day that he'd never even tried." His frown somehow manages to be both sad and angry. "If he'd said from the beginning that he wanted an open relationship, I would probably have agreed, you know? It's not like I was thinking we'd be forever right from the outset—I was only twenty-five, and we'd only known each other a couple of months. Settling down wasn't in my plans when we decided to be exclusive. But he never even mentioned wanting to see other people, and he was the one who brought up monogamy."

"Bastard," I mutter, pressing my hands harder against the ground. I need nature right now, because Felix's story is knotting up my insides, dragging my memories of Alan back to the forefront of my mind. Eoin's not like that—he'd never deliberately deceive me. I *know* he's sticking to our monogamy agreement.

"He deserved broken windows," Jared agrees. "That kind of deliberate dishonesty doesn't belong in relationships."

"Right? It was the lying that hurt the most. The whole time we were together, he was lying to me, over and over." Felix swallows hard and looks away. "When I confronted him, he *laughed*. It was all a joke to him. He said he'd been waiting years for me to find out and he couldn't believe how stupid I was."

The wordless sound that explodes from me clashes with Jared's angry, "Fuck that!"

"It's not stupid to trust your boyfriend," I snap. "He's a malicious prick."

Jared points at me. "What he said. The cheating was bad enough, but the rest just makes him a bad person. I'm glad you trashed his car. Too bad he didn't have a boat too."

There's a stunned silence as Felix and I process that decidedly violent statement from our pacifist friend, and then he snorts a laugh. I bite my lip, not wanting Jared to think we're laughing at him.

"What?" he demands. "Just because I live by the edict to do no harm doesn't mean I can't recognize when other people deserve to have their boats trashed."

That does it. I laugh so hard, I fall backward into the clover, while Felix sounds like he's choking. But the time I can breathe again, my eyes are wet with tears. I swipe them away and stare up into the endless blue of the sky, still chuckling lightly, letting go of the painful knot of memories. Alan is in my past and no longer merits my hurt. My concerns about Eoin don't have anything to do with him cheating or deceiving me.

Something nudges against my arm, and I roll my head to the side and smile. "Hello, sweetheart," I croon to Elsking, scooping her onto my chest and stroking her soft fur. "Did I startle you? I didn't mean to."

She doesn't seem upset at all, sniffing around my shirt for a moment before she jumps back down and heads for the sage plants nearby. I sit up so I can keep an eye on her, and my gaze lands on Jared's self-satisfied smile.

"You said that on purpose," I accuse, and he shrugs.

"Of course. How would I have said it accidentally?"

That's not what I meant, but I let it go. He's a natural caretaker, so I shouldn't be surprised that he wanted to lighten our moods.

Felix must agree, because he says, "On purpose or accident, thanks. I needed that." He seems to have let his guard down, making him look a lot younger, and I remember what he said earlier and do a quick calculation.

"You're only forty-two?"

He blinks at me. "Yeah. Why? How old are you?"

I shake my head. "More than a hundred times older than you. Sorry, I didn't mean to be rude—I just thought you were older, for some reason." I try to remember what I know about shifter maturity. "Were you even considered an adult when all that shit happened with your ex?"

"Why wouldn't he have been? He was... what? Twenty-eight or so," Jared says, frowning, then glances at Felix. "Right? That's what you said. You met when you were twenty-five and were together three years."

He nods. "Yeah, I was. Dáithí might be confusing adulthood with reproductive maturity, which happens when we go through our second puberty."

The way Jared's jaw drops makes me wish I'd been recording. "What?"

"Shifters don't go through puberty until they're around forty," I tell him. I can't even remember how I found that out, so it's not surprising that Jared, who only learned about the community this year and has been focused on us elves, not the other species, doesn't know.

"Reproductive puberty," Felix corrects. "We go through puberty at the same time as the other species, too, as we develop into adulthood, but it's less intense. The theory is that learning to control our shift is already hard enough without adding reproductive hormones. That happens in our late thirties or early forties, when we're adults and better equipped to handle it."

"Wow. That's... wow." Jared's eyes narrow. "Is that why you're so aggressive on the ice? Hormones? Has your puberty finished yet?"

I cough. "Whoa, Jared. That's *me* levels of nosy."

His expression turns apologetic, but Felix waves him off. "I don't care. No, it's not finished yet—I'm a late bloomer. It's made things really hard lately."

It's an effort to keep a straight face and not say, "That's what he said." Things being hard during puberty? It's the perfect time for a dick joke.

But I'm proud of my mature restraint when he continues, "I'll admit to being more annoyed than usual lately, but I've always been an aggressive player, and I just dialed it up when I realized it was the only way to hold my own against the bigger guys on the ice. When I was a teenager, my coaches encouraged it—there's only so many spots on a team roster, and if the bigger guys have talent, they get picked first. If I wanted to play pro, I needed to bring more to the table than everyone else."

"But you're a great player," Jared protests. "You have tons of talent! And the Warhammers is the only team in the league that doesn't have a more even mix of player sizes. You'd still be able to play based on your talent and skills alone."

Based on Felix's face, that's not true, but I don't know enough about hockey to have an opinion. Maybe I should learn about the sport. If Felix and I are going to be friends—and I think we are—I should know a little about what he does. It's friend law.

"Thanks," he says, not sounding convinced. "But I don't want to move away from here, and Coach would cut me if I stopped playing rough."

"He'd *cut* you?" I demand, outraged, and then my knowledge of sports terminology reasserts itself. "Oh. From the team." It's been over a decade since I learned to speak English, but sometimes I still get tripped up. "Would he really? Even if you were still scoring... points?" I'm guessing on that last word.

"Goals," he corrects. "And yeah. He pushes us all to play rougher. It's right on the edge of encouraging us to play dirty—in fact, I'm pretty sure he's crossed that line with some of the guys." Disgust mixes with misery in his tone.

Jared's appalled. "That's disgraceful!"

"Don't get too upset on my behalf," Felix says with a wry smile. "I really am an aggressive player naturally, and Coach never told me to beat up on my own teammates." He winces. "Which is what led to that Ari guy saying I assault people."

"You beat up your teammates?" Now I'm intrigued. "I had no idea hockey was a last-man-standing kind of sport."

"It's not," Jared says firmly while Felix laughs. "Felix gets frustrated with his teammates. That's all."

"Part of it's puberty," Felix agrees. "It's so fucking annoying that some of them are on the team just because of their size, even when they're making sloppy mistakes. I used to deal with it better, but the last few years, hormones have been killing my patience."

"So why haven't they been cut yet? Jared said the other teams have a mix of player sizes. Why are the Warhammers so fixated on big players?"

He shrugs. "That's the way Coach and the old general manager wanted it. I'm not sure if the new GM is the same— too early to tell."

"Your coach sounds like a douchecanoe," I tell him, and he nods.

"Fuck yeah. Any other coach would have suspended me the first time I belted a teammate on the ice, but he just ignores it."

I make a mental note to talk to Eoin about the coach. If the king is going to be around that man, Eoin needs to know what to expect. Maybe I can call hockey Erik and get his take on the new general manager too. We're not friends, but I bet I could sweet-talk him.

"But that's my side of the deal done," Felix continues. "And hey, good news is, I won't have to see my ex or that Ari asshole ever again. Now I want to hear about your complicated boyfriend, Dáithí."

I groan. "I've talked about this way too much lately. The short version is, I had my heart broken in the past by someone whose history is a lot like Eoin's, he and I agreed starting out that we'd keep it casual, but now he wants to change that and he's going to complete a bunch of challenges to prove his commitment."

He stares at me. "I'm going to need the long version."

Of course he does. I tell the whole story—with many interjections and additions from Jared—and every word I say makes it all seem even more ridiculous.

Felix lets out a low whistle when I'm done. "I thought I was fucked-up, but you're giving me a run for my money."

"Hey!" He's not wrong, damn it.

"I'm just saying, that man must seriously want you. For one thing, he's spending his Saturday morning cleaning *your* apartment while you're here bitching with us."

I reach out to where Elsking and Marge are napping and stroke my sweetheart's soft fur. "Yeah." How dare he keep making factual statements that contain valid points?

"That's only a fraction of it," Jared adds. "Did you see the updated progress report last night? Ari says Eoin's been researching custom accessories for Elsking because he doesn't think what she's got is good enough for her. And he told you to bring her so she wouldn't be upset by his cleaning today. He's killing it on the task he doesn't even know about."

"See?" Felix gestures to Jared. "He's not only willing to tackle this stupid challenge, he's *trying*. I don't know the guy, but from what you've told me, he's determined to show you he can be what you want, and you're comparing him to someone who not only didn't try, but blamed you for it afterward." He shakes his head. "There's no guarantees in any relationship, Dáithí. But if you care about someone enough, you risk it anyway."

Ouch. Stung, I demand, "Have you been risking it since your ex screwed you over?"

"Yes," he says bluntly. "A bunch of times. Jared met me the day my last boyfriend broke up with me."

Jared winces. "That's why you threw your phone?"

He nods. "Uh-huh. I've been burned a whole bunch of times, and I'll probably be burned some more, because I'm looking for someone who loves me so much, he'll do whatever it takes to show me." He cocks a brow. "Sound familiar?"

I guess we're friends now, because only a true friend would call me on my bullshit like that.

Damn him.

CHAPTER TWENTY-TWO

Eoin

Dáithí doesn't get back until late in the afternoon, which works out perfectly for me. I had time to clean the whole place from top to bottom, including under the furniture and rugs. I even managed to give the inside of the windows a once-over. His place isn't big—at all—but cleaning it that thoroughly took hours, even using magic to help move things around.

Technically, I had permission to use magic for the whole job, but the standard cleaning spells I already know wouldn't have achieved the outcome I wanted, and it would have taken longer to design new spells than it did to just clean manually. Maybe if this was something I planned to do all the time, like if I was a cleaner or something, it would be worth the time.

By the time I hear the front door open, I'm sacked out on the couch, feet up, brimming with smug satisfaction.

"Eoin?" Dáithí calls.

"I'm in here."

He appears in the doorway a second later, Elsking's carrier in his hand. "Why does it smell like fresh cookies and tréghel leaves?"

"Because you like both those things. It's a room-scenting spell."

The sound he makes is a combination of surprise and delight. "My house is always going to smell like this?"

Shrugging, I get to my feet and go over to kiss him. Nothing will ever be as amazing as the feel of his lips against mine—except maybe that happy smile on his face. "Unless we end the spell, or stop refreshing it. It's good for a couple of years, but it'll need to be touched up at that point."

"Why would I want to end it? You've made my house smell like *home*." He bends over and carefully sets down the crate, then throws his arms around me and squeezes. "How can you know what I need when I don't even know it?" he mumbles against my neck. I wrap him up in my hold and breathe in the precious scent of him.

When he finally lifts his head and presses a kiss to my jaw, his smile is back. "Okay, you've managed to make the place smell amazing, and the little bit I've seen so far is cleaner than it's ever been before, probably including when it was brand-new. Let me put Elsking in her hutch, and you can wow me with the rest."

I let him go and wait for him to—

"Fuck me, what did you do to the hutch?"

—see the changes I made. "Is it okay?" I don't think he'll be mad, but I probably should have checked with him. I figured it would be fine, since he dotes on Elsking.

"Is it okay? Are you really asking me if it's okay that you built an extension for Elsking's hutch and added what looks like a super cool multi-level playground made of tunnels?"

It's hard to tell if he's mad with the incredulous surprise still so strong in his voice. "Yeah."

He laughs. "Of course it's okay! Eoin, it's incredible—she's going to love it. I can't believe you did this." He opens the gate of the carrier and scoops Elsking out, then sets her carefully in the hutch. We both watch as she takes a moment to get her bearings, then cautiously sniffs around where I took out the back wall and added more space and the tunnel system.

"The assistant at the hardware store walked me through it when I went to get the stuff for the new spice rack." I don't tell him why I was asking about it in the first place—I want to do more research first and make sure I have all the facts. And if it turns out my concerns are unfounded, no harm done. Elsking will still be able to enjoy the extra space.

"It's perfect," Dáithí assures me as Elsking crawls into the first tunnel. "Thank you." He loops an arm around my waist and leans against me. "I don't deserve you."

Alarm explodes through me, and even though I try not to show it, I can't stop my body from stiffening. "Dáithí—"

He straightens and forces a smile. "Don't worry about it."

"I think I will, though, because that sounded like the kind of thing someone says right before breaking up." I study his face, but he's giving nothing away. "You agreed to give me this chance, and I'm not done with the tasks." Even as I say the words, I'm aware of how empty they are. If Dáithí really wants to end us and walk away, I can't—won't—force him to stay. The challenge is only valid if we both want to be here, trying to make things work.

His shrug is tiny, but somehow... reassuring? "I'm not backing out, Eoin."

Okay. That's good. Then why... "You don't actually think you don't deserve me, do you?"

He must hear the disbelief in my tone, because his smile reappears and his eyes go soft as he lifts a hand to my cheek. I turn my head to kiss his fingers. "I think it's more complicated than that. It was pointed out to me today that I haven't exactly been fair to you."

"I suggested—"

"Yeah, but—"

"Dáithí, we're both—"

"Okay, stop!" He's laughing now, and it eases me to see it. "I don't want to argue about this. Just know that I'm fully aware of how awesome you are, and I'm trying to get over myself."

My mind flashes back to what Ari said the other week about Dáithí having been hurt in the past. Maybe I didn't give that as much weight as I should have—I was so sure Dáithí would have mentioned it, but it could have been too painful to talk about.

Because if it's not *me* that's keeping him from making a commitment, it has to be him, right? Why else would he say he needs to "get over himself"? And I've known him long enough to have seen him in relationships before, so it's not that he's got commitment issues... which leaves past trauma. Something that hurt him so deeply, he doesn't like to talk about it much.

I make a mental note to discreetly ask around and see what I can find out. In the meantime... "Who said you haven't been fair? Jared?" I hope not. Me yelling at my boss's boyfriend isn't something I ever wanted to do.

Relief flashes across his face, and I file that away to think about later too. "Not Jared, Felix. My new bestie, which means he's allowed to say stuff like that." He pats my chest. "Now, show me the rest of the place. Let's start with the spice rack."

"I'm just saying, it's ridiculous that even our Uber driver knows where we're going, but I still don't," Dáithí argues. He's been saying variations of the same thing for the past twenty minutes, and I smile and nod just like I have every other time. It wins me a glare, but he's not really mad. If anything, he's excited by all the secrecy.

I hope this date lives up to the hype.

"You're sure I'm dressed right?" he asks. "If I'm not because you didn't tell me what our destination was, I'll never let it go, you know that, right?"

"I know, and you're dressed right." I lean in and murmur against his ear, "You look incredibly fuckable." It's true—I told him to dress sexy for going out, and he did—but what puts it over the top is knowing what he's wearing underneath those jeans that are so tight, he had to lie down to get them on.

He flicks me a flirty glance through his lashes and lays a hand high on my thigh. "You say the sweetest things... but that one's true."

I chuckle as the car slows, and then our driver pulls over and stops at the curb.

"This is as close as I can get without double-parking," he says apologetically. "Is that okay?"

Glancing out the window, I assure him it is, then tip and thank him as Dáithí and I slide out. Our destination is three doors up, but even from here it's obvious what it is.

"A club?" He turns an excited smile to me. "We're going dancing?"

"We're going dancing," I confirm, looping an arm around him and steering him along the street. "Three guesses who the guest DJ is tonight."

"It's someone I'd know? Hm, okay... Wait, community or human?" He glances around to make sure nobody overheard, but we're close enough to the club now that noise from the people in line mingles with the music spilling from inside and makes eavesdropping hard.

"Community. This is a community club—a community *queer* club."

His face lights up with the understanding that he can fully relax tonight without having to be on guard against bigots or slipping up in front of unknowing humans.

"You're seriously gifted when it comes to planning dates, Eoin. Okay, a community DJ that I'd know…" His eyes go wide. "It's not Adjoa K?"

I wink, and the sound he makes can only be called a squeal. "*How?* I thought she was in Europe for the rest of the summer?"

"There you are!" Hagen bounces up to us before I have to come up with an answer to Dáithí's question. "Finally! We've been waiting forever." He gestures toward a group of people, and Dáithí glances in that direction, then looks up at me.

"You invited friends?"

For a split second, I wonder if it was the wrong decision and he would have preferred it to be just us. Then he pulls me in for a big, wet kiss, and I mentally pat myself on the back for getting it right.

"Thank you! Clubbing is so much more fun with a group." He abandons my side to say hi to the others, a mix of friends from work and outside of it, and Hagen slaps me on the shoulder.

"Dude, you just got here, and I can already tell you got points for this one."

My gaze follows Dáithí, who's jabbing a finger at Ari for reasons I can only guess at. "I hope so."

"Pfft. I know so. It's never been a secret that he loves to dance. This would have been a winner even without all the extra bells and whistles you added."

"Maybe, but it's worth it anyway."

He rolls his eyes and hauls me over to the group. "Come on, we're all here now. Let's get inside. The bouncer wouldn't let us in without you."

"We're all on the guest list?" Dáithí asks, turning away

from Ari, who looks relieved. "How did you get tickets to Adjoa K for such a big group?"

"Eoin sprang for bottle service," Caoimhe says before I can stop her, and Dáithí's jaw drops.

"For all of us?"

"I got a discount," I excuse, then make for the door before he can ask why. The bouncer eyes me with jaded weariness until I tell him my name and show ID, and then he's all smiles, radioing for someone to come and meet us and ushering us inside.

Even though it's early and the opening DJ is still playing, the club is already packed wall-to-wall with bodies. Our server leads us upstairs to the VIP section, which is warded to reduce the noise level and where we have two booths reserved. Within five minutes, our first bottles have been opened and poured. For a little while, we drink and talk, and with Dáithí pressed up against my side and the distant vibration of the bass, it's easy to relax. We should do this more often—not the VIP thing, though I can't deny I like it, but getting out with friends. This is something I enjoy, and fuck knows Dáithí loves it, so why has it taken the challenge for me to make it happen?

"Let's dance," I say to Dáithí, suddenly determined not to waste a second of this night. I toss back the remainder of the champagne in my glass.

He grins at me and follows suit, and then we race each other down the stairs to the crowded dance floor.

Being pressed up against Dáithí is always my idea of a good time. Pressed up against him while he moves to the beat, head thrown back, exulting in the music?

Fucking outstanding.

CHAPTER TWENTY-THREE

Dáithí

How is dancing with hundreds of other people in a hot, too-small space one of the most transcendental experiences a person can have? Logically, it makes no sense, but when I'm crammed onto a dance floor and the music takes me over, every stress I have disappears. My mind clears, and for a short time, I understand what it means to be one with the universe. It's always been that way, even back home. Even when the dance floor was a clearing in a tréghel forest.

The only other thing that can get me to that place is good sex, but it's different. When I dance, it's just me there, even if I'm surrounded by others. Sex shares the experience with another person—which is probably why not every orgasm can get me there. Opening your soul to merge with existence makes you vulnerable beyond the physical, and I wouldn't want that with every person I've fucked.

I might be drunk. Merging with existence isn't something I usually think about, whether via dancing or sex.

Throwing my arms around Eoin's neck, I press my whole body against his and shout, "I always merge with the universe when you fuck me!"

He makes a confused face and shakes his head. "I can't hear you properly," he yells back, and I make the executive decision that it's time for another break from dancing. I need to piss anyway.

Grabbing his hand, I begin pushing through the crowd toward the stairs, and it only takes Eoin a second to catch on and move ahead of me. He's not *that* much bigger than me, but somehow people react like he's seven feet tall and three feet wide, parting easily to let him through. I take advantage of it, but that doesn't mean I don't resent them for not doing the same for me. Don't they understand the power I have?

"I could cut them off from the good printer!" I proclaim as we reach the velvet rope at the bottom of the stairs. Eoin and the bouncer stationed there both look at me, Eoin with fondness, the bouncer with an eye roll. Clearly he doesn't understand how much power I have either.

He does see our wristbands, though, and unhooks the rope to let us through. The stairs are swaying just enough to make walking up them a challenge, but Eoin puts a hand on my back to guide me. He's the best.

"I'm having such a great time," I tell him. "Bathroom break, more drinks because my mouth's dry, and then back to dancing." It's already nearly two, and I'm determined to make the most of every minute we have before closing.

"You're the boss."

I pause on the steps to give him a sexy smirk. "I like being the boss of you, but sometimes it's fun for you to be the boss of me."

His gaze darkens, and he steals a kiss. "I like it both ways. Maybe when you're sober we can talk about it some more."

"Yes! You can sober me up when we get home and then we can fuck till we pass out." Talk about the perfect end to the perfect night.

Eoin chuckles and nudges me to get started up the stairs

again. "Sure, baby. What were you saying downstairs? I don't think I heard it right."

I said something downstairs? Oh! "When you fuck me, I always merge with the universe."

The sudden dead silence is my first hint that we've stepped through the ward at the top of the stairs. My second hint is the laughter that breaks out. I guess everyone in the VIP area heard me.

"We could have timed that better," Eoin says, but he doesn't sound mad, and he's grinning.

"Oops?" We head toward our tables, where a few of our friends are—most are downstairs.

"Merge with the universe?" Ari asks, his face alight with laughter. "Is that a euphemism?"

I slide into the seat across from him, pulling Eoin down beside me, and jab a finger in his direction. "You only wish you could make someone come that hard. Which reminds me, I'm still mad at you."

"How do those two things connect?" Eoin wonders out loud, waving our server off as she comes to see if we need anything. Our latest bottle—the third for our table—isn't empty yet, and last time we came back up, we ordered a couple of rounds of other drinks too. One of mine is still half full, and I pick it up and take a sip now.

"You can't just go around accusing people of things," I continue, shaking my head. "And definitely you can't accuse my friends of things. It's rude, Ari, and I'm so ashamed of you."

"He wasn't your friend until this morning," Ari mutters.

"That's irrev—ivver—irrerel— It's not the point!"

"Irrelevant," Eoin murmurs, and I pat his arm in thanks. "What are we talking about, exactly? Why are you mad, and is this one of those situations when I should be mad, too, or are you handling it?"

Aww. "You are so merging me later. I'm gonna make you merge me so hard."

"So it *is* a euphemism." Ari leaps to change the subject. "But before it seemed like fucking and merging were—"

"Don't try to distract us. Eoin needs to know how rude you are." I turn my attention to Eoin. "Ari was rude to my friend Felix."

Eoin looks at me expectantly—I'm not sure why—and then glances across the table at Ari. "Care to add anything?"

Sulkily folding his arms across his chest, Ari says, "No, thanks. You've already reamed me out about it."

Did I always know Eoin was sexy when he frowned? There's this little crease right between his eyes that screams for me to lick it.

"I— Wait, is this about what happened in the meeting with the Warhammers? Your friend Felix is that Felix?"

"Of course. Who else would he be?" Dammit, the crease disappeared. I'll have to lick it another time.

"I didn't know you even knew him. How did you meet?"

"We're getting off topic, which is that Ari was mean and hurtful." I reach for the champagne bottle. If we're going to keep talking, I need to wet my throat.

"Jared introduced them," Ari says. "Apparently he and Ansas are buddies, which nobody bothered to tell me before."

"Felix Ansas is the player Jared knows?"

"Why is everyone surprised about that? Didn't you ask Jared what his friend's name was?" I did.

They both look embarrassed. Guess they didn't think of that.

"We're not getting off topic," Eoin tells me. "I've already made it clear to Ari that he needs to be more diplomatic. He's sorry for what he said."

"But why did he—" I twist back around to face Ari. "Why

did you say it? Not all the parts about his ex, but saying he attacks people was just mean."

Ari's mouth presses into a flat line. "It's true, though. He goes after his teammates on the ice—I've seen videos of it."

"He's not proud of it! And it's partly his coach's fault anyway." There's a flaw in that argument, something my brain doesn't like, but I refuse to be distracted by logic and reason. "Why, Ari? *Why?*"

"I don't know, okay?" He runs one hand through his hair and grabs his drink with the other. "Something about him just pushed my buttons. I'm sorry."

I narrow my eyes on him. "Have you told him that?"

"Told him what?"

"That you're sorry?"

"Dáithí," Eoin begins, but Ari cuts him off.

"No. Because during the meeting wasn't the right time and I'm not ever going to see him again."

It's my turn to fold my arms. "He's my friend and you're Eoin's friend—and sometimes mine—so you're going to see each other again. I refuse to have an awkward friendship circle, which means you have to say sorry and make it better."

"We're only friends sometimes?" He sounds hurt by that, and I instantly feel bad.

"Most of the time. When you're not being..." I wave my hand toward him, encompassing the vibes he's giving tonight.

"When I'm not being me? Do you understand what he means?" he asks Eoin.

"Yes, but that's not as important as the fact that he's right. You need to apologize to Ansas."

Ari throws up his hands. "If I ever run into him at your place or whatever, I will. I promise not to make the friend-ship circle awkward. Can we be friends, now?"

I nod. "That's acceptable to me." Since that's sorted, I need to find the bathroom. My bladder's reached its limit.

Eoin shakes his head. "No, you need to contact him and apologize in your role as a member of the security team."

I instantly forget about my bladder. "What? Why?"

"What he said," Ari adds.

"Because you're going to be the liaison with the Warhammers for this project, including the training camp visit."

"Dáithí!"

I lift my head and glare at Alistair. Shouting like that in my reception area is not okay.

"How come I didn't get invited out on the weekend?" he demands, plonking his elbows on the raised part of the desk and leaning forward. "We're friends! I'm on your support team! This was a Summit of Love event!"

"Is this really the best use of your Monday morning?"

He pouts. "Noah told me to get out of the office until I was ready to quit complaining."

Noah's a smart man. "So you thought you'd come and complain here and ruin the afterglow of my amazing weekend?"

"Now you're rubbing it in that I missed out? Wow, Dáithí. That's mean."

I give up. "Eoin made the guest list. I didn't know anything about it until we arrived. Take it up with him."

He nods enthusiastically. "Oh, I will. But first..." Glancing around, he leans so far over the desk that I worry he might somersault into my lap. "Give me a status update."

"Not this again." Most of my irritation is due to the unsettled feelings I've been having over the past few days. I need to work through them and decide what I actually want, but I've been putting it off because the high of the weekend was too good to ruin... which means I also feel guilty about putting it off for selfish reasons. My head is an exhausting place to be today.

Alistair gives me big puppy eyes, and I sigh. Unless and until I end this challenge, he and the others are entitled to updates. "What do you want to know, exactly?"

"This was the second date, right? Hagen said he also cleaned your apartment. How did that go?"

"It was perfect," I admit, remembering the joy of making pancakes yesterday and not having to rummage for five minutes to find the cinnamon. "Totally clean and organized, but he didn't mess with my stuff. I still know where everything is." A smile tugs at my mouth. "He built an extension for Elsking's hutch with a playground for her, and he used a spell to make the house smell like my favorite things."

Alistair makes a humming noise. "So he gets full points for that task, and points toward the living entity one?"

"Yeah. All the points." My chest tightens. "Hey, Alistair? How would you have felt if your boyfriend asked you to do all this?"

He makes a weird face. Is he trying to raise his brows? Why is his face scrunching like that?

"Are you second-guessing the Summit of Love?"

My eye twitches, but I let that stupid name pass. "No. Maybe. I'm... just curious." It's the most unconvincing thing I've ever said, but he answers the question anyway.

"Honestly, it would depend why he asked it. If it was an ego thing, or just to make me jump through hoops, I'd walk away. I don't want to be in that kind of relationship, and thankfully Aidan doesn't either. He'd never ask me to." He shrugs, even as my stomach sinks. Is this whole thing just going to convince Eoin I'm not who he wants, after all?

"But," Alistair continues, "if Aidan had something going on in his life and needed me to give him some extra reassurance, then I'd do anything he wanted."

Which sounds good, but Eoin has no idea why I'm so reluctant to believe he can make this commitment. As far as he's concerned, I really might be doing this for an ego trip. "Yeah. I guess."

"It's like, when I was young, my boyfriend tried to burn down my house with me in it."

What?

"That made me leery about having another boyfriend," he goes on, like he didn't just say something completely unhinged. "Aidan understood that, and he helped me get past it." He tips his head to the side and purses his lips. It looks ridiculous. "Not that it took much for me to get past it, but he still helped."

"Is this your way of saying I should talk to Eoin about things that might be holding me back?"

He holds up his hands. "You asked how I'd feel, so I'm giving you context. That's all. I'll email the others and we can schedule a time for a full debrief. Eoin's making big progress, so we should try to keep up."

I make an agreeing noise as he turns away, but he's barely taken three steps before he turns back. "Hey, Dáithí? Don't forget that you never asked Eoin to do any of this. It was his idea."

CHAPTER TWENTY-FOUR

Eoin

SATURDAY NIGHT MIGHT HAVE BEEN a raving success—I know it was because Dáithí told me—but that hasn't stopped Dáithí from being a little subdued all week. I'm worried that it's related to what he said on Saturday about not deserving me, but he's not receptive to talking about it. The last time I asked, he said he wanted time to work out what his own thoughts were.

Between that, getting a little ahead on my regular work so I can spend today on reception, and Ari's newfound determination to annoy me until I fire him so he won't have to work with the Warhammers, it's been a chaotic week. But I'm ready for this. I've looked through the training manual Candice from CSG loaned me, and Dáithí left a cheat sheet for me on his desk. I was a soldier for thousands of years, involved in complex operations to protect and relocate people in the midst of a widespread catastrophic series of events. For part of that time, I was in charge of some of those operations. I've been running Raðulfr's security for the last few hundred years—I deal with his viceroys and other heads of state as a matter of routine. I'm pretty sure I can handle reception for the day.

And Ari's just going to have to suck it up and quit being a baby. I assigned him to the king yesterday so he could sulk out all his feelings while being useful. Hopefully he's back to himself today, because it's up to him to manage the team while I'm preoccupied with this.

"This" being the meeting room schedule. I came in early so I'd have time to read through the cheat sheet and familiarize myself with everything, but I didn't anticipate the meeting room schedule. Dáithí's list says to check which rooms have been booked and whether the booking is for an internal meeting or if there will be visitors attending. If there are visitors coming, I need to confirm that they're already on the visitor list, and if not add their name, who their contact is, and check whether they'll need to sign in so they can go through the security gate—and if so, there's a whole list of other things I need to check off. I'm familiar with that list, though, seeing as I helped Steffen Draco write it and talked him down when he wanted to include biometric scanning as a requirement.

It should be fairly simple. After all, the process for booking a meeting room requires staff to include these details, and the process for having a visitor in the office requires them to do the rest. Even if they forget to note visitor names when booking the meeting room, they should already be on the visitor list—or vice versa.

The problem seems to be that we work with people who are incapable of following a basic process.

I click into every single taken slot on the schedule. There are eight rooms, with sixteen potential half-hour meeting slots available for each room. Almost three quarters of them are taken, and only six have all the necessary information.

Sucking an annoyed breath in through my nose, I scroll

back to the nine o'clock slot and start noting down who I'll need to contact. Thankfully, a lot of the bookings span multiple time slots, which cuts the number of meetings I need to chase up even further. But I'm going to have *quite* a lot to say to these people.

I send a message to everyone whose meetings begin after ten, but I'll have to call the ones that start at nine. This is such a waste of my time—there are still three things on Dáithí's list that I need to do before the office is open to visitors in twenty minutes. I stab the digits for the first extension into the keypad.

"What?"

I pull the handset away from my ear and look at it. What the fuck?

"Hanesty?" I check. Usually he answers the phone with his name, but even if he's trying something new, "what" is not it.

"Who's this? Is Dáithí not in today?"

My eyes narrow. He thought it was Dáithí, and he answered the phone like that? "It's Eoin. I'm filling in for Dáithí today."

There's a thudding sound that might be Hanesty dropping something, and it gives me dark satisfaction.

"Eoin! You're... wow. Okay. Couldn't get a temp at the last minute, hey?"

I don't bother to reply. I've already wasted too much time on him. "You've booked Meeting Room 3 at nine o'clock but haven't followed the process. Update the booking information or I'll cancel it."

"The... oh, uh. Really? I didn't think we actually needed to do that."

"What was it that made you think that? The fact that a process document was created for it, or the instructions that pop up when you click into the schedule to make a booking?"

He gives a strained, nervous laugh. "No, I mean, visitors check in with Dáithí anyway, right? So it doesn't need to be in the booking."

Does he realize he's talking to the head of the king's personal security right now, openly stating that he doesn't follow security practices for the office where the king works?

"Update it in the next two minutes or I'm canceling the booking. And since it sounds like you have external people coming, they'd better be on the visitor list." I end the call before I have to listen to him say anything else. If you'd asked me ten minutes ago, I would have said Hanesty was decent enough and not the type to make trouble.

I'm currently reassessing that opinion.

Mentioning the visitor list raised another concern, though, and before I make the next call, I bring up that file—and swear. I can't be certain that people haven't been populating it, but I do know approximately how much traffic comes through this office every day, and based on that there should be a lot more names on this list.

Is this the kind of bullshit Dáithí deals with before he even needs to switch the external phone lines to active?

Making a snap decision, I stab the buttons on the phone, dialing an extension that's not on my list. It takes less than a minute to explain the situation to Steffen—I don't even need to finish before he turns growly and demands I let him deal with it—and then I snap a photo of my list and text it to him.

If people are going to fuck around, they're going to find out.

"JUST FUCKING DO what you're supposed to, you motherfucking piece of shit!" My shout bounces off the walls of the small room, and the very young marketing assistant who asked for my help slowly backs toward the door. I suck in a deep breath—something I've done too many times already in the past hour and fourteen minutes—and resist the urge to kick the damn printer. I'm pretty sure it won't help.

It would make me feel better, though.

I'm on deep breath number three before I manage to calm down enough to paste on a smile... though from the look on the marketing assistant's face, it's more of a grimace. "Just leave it with me," I promise them. "You said you needed the reports for a meeting this afternoon, right?"

Wide-eyed, they nod.

"Great! Come back at noon, and they'll be ready for you." I'm not sure how convinced they are, but they manage to squeak a thank-you before racing away. I go back to the reception desk, where there are now even more fucking incoming call lights on the phone, plus three people waiting. I must've talked to fifty people already today, and it's not even ten yet. How am I supposed to get the things on the list done?

Ignoring the phones—the calls go into a hold queue if they're not answered immediately—I look at the first person waiting. "Welcome to the DEA." My voice is a lot less welcoming than Dáithí's usually is, but I can't help that right now. "How can I help you?"

"I've got an appointment with Asha Carse. I'm Kari Pelen." She smiles, and the smile I give in return is a lot more natural this time, thanks to the magic Steffen worked with the meeting schedule and visitor list. Her name is right where it's supposed to be, with all the relevant information attached, as is the name of the man next in line. I tell them both to have a seat, send messages to let the respective employees know, then turn my attention to the third person. A delivery guy—what a relief. Finally something easy to handle.

"Need me to sign for that?" I nod toward the courier envelope under his arm.

He frowns and looks around, then shifts his weight from one foot to the other. "Is Dáithí on break? I might wait for him to get back."

Hagen's words from a few weeks back spring into my memory. *"I heard the delivery guy ask Dáithí if he's seeing anyone..."* This delivery guy? This guy's been flirting with *my* guy?

My expression must change, because he races to add, "No shade to you, man. I just don't know you, and these are sensitive documents, you know?"

"I work here," I point out icily. "Do you know every person you deliver documents to?"

He stutters for a very long few seconds, then looks around again and leans forward conspiratorially. "I swear, I'm not insulting you. I just wanna talk to Dáithí, yeah? I haven't had a delivery here all week, so this is the first chance I've had since last Wednesday."

I'd probably lose points on this task if I ripped this guy's arms off, so I tamp down on the urge and say, "Oh?"

He nods. "I've been trying to get his attention for months, and I think I've finally got a shot. But I'd get fired if I asked for his number while I'm working—not professional, you know? So I gotta cram my work into these deliveries."

He thinks he has a *shot*? My fingers start to tingle with offensive magic I've used so many times, I don't even need to remember the spell.

"Hey, Eoin!" Hagen's shout precedes the security gate opening and him jogging into reception, followed by Ari and Caolan. He skids to a halt beside the soon-to-be-armless delivery guy and gives me a hard look. "Got a second?"

I consciously let go of the spell, pulling myself back into control. Dáithí would be super mad if I disgraced his job by attacking someone—even this douche who thinks he has a shot.

"Yeah." I hold out my hand for the envelope. "Dáithí's not in today. Sorry."

The guy's face falls. "Bummer." Sighing, he taps the screen of his device and offers it to me. "Could you sign here with your finger?"

A minute later, I have the envelope and he's gone. I toss it onto the desk and drop into Dáithí's chair, burying my face in my hands. "Fuck."

"That's one word for it," Ari agrees, sounding way too gleeful. "Lucky Hagen recognized him. It would have been so unprofessional for you to have punched a courier."

That brings my head up, and I glare at him. "I wasn't going to punch him. But even if I had, there would have been more reason for it than there was for you to be an ass in that meeting."

"You weren't going to punch him?" Caolan asks. "Really? Because if someone who was flirting with David was suddenly two feet away from me and gave me a reason to, I... might." He glances around furtively. "Don't tell him. It's not reasonable."

"I wasn't going to punch him," I repeat, and when all three of them look deeply skeptical, I add, "I was going to rip his arms off."

CHAPTER TWENTY-FIVE

Eoin

HAGEN TSKS, but he's grinning. "So violent. What did he say, anyway? One minute you were just freaked out, and then the next you were freaked out and mad. We got here just as you transitioned to homicidal."

I don't want to admit that I got mad just from realizing the guy has a thing for Dáithí—as Caolan said, it's not reasonable—so I mutter, "He said he has a shot with Dáithí." Then I wince. That doesn't sound reasonable either, when I say it out loud. Before Ari can make another smartass comment, I continue, "Were you watching me? What the fuck?"

"From the surveillance room," Ari confirms cheerfully. "Someone has to keep track of how you're doing to tell Dáithí later."

"You're supposed to be managing the team while I'm here." Not that the team needs to be micromanaged, but if he's closed away in the surveillance room—which is mostly a closet with the backend of the CCTV equipment and a couple of monitors—then he's not exactly accessible if they do need him.

He holds up his phone. "They know how to reach me, and

I only left the office twenty minutes ago. I'd be gone longer for a meeting."

True, but...

Hagen smirks. "Still the same old control freak. Don't worry about your team—worst-case scenario, they know where to find you. I'm kind of surprised they haven't been taking turns to come out and spy on you."

I'm sure they would, which is why I forbade it on pain of being assigned to do background checks for the rest of the year. Ari opens his mouth—probably to say so—but reconsiders and closes it when I narrow my eyes. He's still dealing with the aftermath of the last background checks I assigned to him.

"Unlike you, they have better work ethic than that," I tell Hagen, making him laugh out loud. We both know there's nothing wrong with his work ethic, but when you were roommates with someone for hundreds of years, you're allowed to casually insult them. It's an unwritten law.

"How have things been going?" he asks, and I scoff.

"You've been watching, so I'm sure we all agree that I won't be replacing Dáithí full-time."

"That's not the point of this task," Caolan reminds me.

"I'm still not sure what the point of this task *is*." I've been trying to understand it, but the best I've come up with is that it's testing my commitment to do *anything* to prove myself to Dáithí, which doesn't seem like something he'd agree to. He's not shallow like that, and he takes his job seriously.

"That's okay, we do." Ari still sounds way too cheerful. If he keeps this up, I'm going to tell Erik that we want to expand the collaboration plans. "Is the phone supposed to be flashing like that?"

I glance down at the phone, which has lights flashing on all four external lines and several internal ones. "Shit." I check that my Bluetooth headset is connected, then jab the button for one of the external ones. The people who work here can get off their asses and come see me if they need something. "Welcome to the DEA. How may I direct your call?"

Ten frustrating minutes later, there are no external calls waiting and most of the internal ones have dropped off too. Bonus: I only accidentally hung up on one person. It's not my fault that the Transfer button is right beside the End Call button. That was a stupid design choice.

Slumping back in the chair, I turn my attention back to my friends, who are still standing around like we don't all have actual jobs. No wonder Dáithí's so quick to pull out the spray bottle—I would be too, if I had to sit here every day while other people loitered in my space, being annoying.

Speaking of, where is the spray bottle? It's not in its usual spot on the desk. I open a couple of drawers, but it's not there either. Dáithí must have stashed it somewhere for safe-keeping.

Too bad.

"Do any of you need anything? If not, go away. There are shockingly few people here right now, and I have to get through more things on the list while I can."

"Huh," Ari says. "I guess it's true that people who are in relationships start to sound like their partners, because that's something Dáithí would say."

I flip him the bird. There are some things I've learned since coming to Earth that are incredibly useful.

"Do you need anything?" Caolan asks seriously... though he has his phone out and appears to be taking notes. Based on my experience so far today, I doubt they're positive.

"No, I— Wait. Do any of you know how to make the big printer work?"

Caolan takes a step back. "Not me."

"Fuck, no," Hagen agrees, and Ari just shakes his head.

"Great." I check my notes for the number I need, then make a call. "Candice? It's Eoin. I need help with the printer, please." Saying it feels like accepting defeat, but thousands of years of combat experience have taught me that sometimes, you need to assess a situation and cut your losses. I've already spent fifteen minutes trying to make that damn machine do its job, and I've exceeded my very limited knowledge on the subject. It's not likely that I'll get it working on my own, and any time I spend trying will be wasted while people and calls wait out here. I might not be out to get a full-time receptionist job, but Dáithí runs this place efficiently, and I refuse to tarnish that reputation completely. The marketing team *will* get the reports for their meeting, and people who enter or call the DEA *will* be greeted and assisted.

I'm going to manage this if it kills me.

Candice promises she'll be up in ten minutes, and I thank her before ending the call. There's still nobody new waiting, no more calls, and I realize with a whole lot of relief that I've reached what Dáithí calls "the midmorning lull." Thank fuck.

"It seems like you have this under control," Caolan begins, but I shake my head.

"Could you wait here for a few minutes? I need to make a personal call real quick. If the phone rings or someone comes, just say hello and ask them to wait." I got the text earlier, and I only have limited time to follow up before I lose my chance.

The three of them exchange glances. "Okay," Caolan says at last, coming around the desk and looking dubiously at the phone. "Do I need the headset?"

I point to the handset. "You can use that if you need to—I swear I won't be long, and I'm not going far." In fact, I'm not even leaving reception. I grab my cell and hit to dial as I pace toward the elevators.

It's answered on the first ring.

"Rescue, Bobby speaking."

"Hi, Bobby. It's Eoin, returning your—"

"Eoin! Great timing—I was going to give it another ten minutes and then call the next name on my list."

I blow out a breath. "It's been a chaotic morning, but I'm glad I got you before you had to."

"So you want her, then?"

"Yes, please. Your message said she's healthy?"

"A little underweight, but otherwise fit as a fiddle," he confirms.

Perfect. "I'll be by tonight, if that's okay? Around six thirty." The office officially closes to visitors at five thirty, plus a few minutes to make sure everything's in order for when Dáithí's back tomorrow, and then I'll need to check in with my team and make sure I don't have any time-sensitive emails.

"No problem. I'll be off shift by then, but Darren will have all the details."

When I return to the desk, relieved that at least one thing is going my way today, I'm met by three curious faces.

"Sooooo..." Ari raises a brow.

"None of your business." Has he always been this nosy?

"Dude, you know I love you like a brother, right?" Hagen asks. "Because it's as your honorary brother that I'm telling you that call sounded weird. Like, call enforcement levels of weird."

I blink at him, barely noticing as Caolan gets out of Dáithí's chair and circles back around to the public side of the desk. "What? It did not." I replay the call in my head. Okay, so... "Only if you have a depraved criminal mind."

"Or have dealt with depraved criminals in the past," he counters. "What was it about?"

I sigh and lean against the raised part of the desk. "When I was building the extension to Elsking's hutch, I—"

"Elsking's the rabbit Dáithí got, right?" Caolan interrupts.

"Yes. Anyway, I found out that rabbits are pretty social. They don't always do well on their own, and they usually thrive when they have friends. So I started asking around at a bunch of rescues for them to let me know if they got any rabbits." I shrug, a little uncomfortable.

Hagen's mouth has dropped open. "You've been trying to find a friend for Dáithí's pet rabbit?"

"Well... yeah. She doesn't deserve to be lonely."

"Um..." Ari screws up his face. "Isn't it uncool to assume Dáithí even wants another pet? What if he doesn't?"

I wave it off. "No, that's fine—I'm the one adopting this bunny. If Dáithí's okay with having another pet in the house, she can live with Elsking, but I've already got a hutch ready at my place in case he'd rather not. They can still have playdates. It might be better to start out that way anyway, so they can get used to each other before they have to share space."

Caolan's smiling. "You have a hutch?" He types something into his phone.

"It would be irresponsible of me to adopt a pet without making sure it has what it needs."

"Let me get this clear," Hagan starts, shaking his head. "You're so worried that Dáithí's rabbit *might* be lonely that you're going to commit to pet ownership yourself so they can have playdates?"

Why do I feel like that's a trick question? "Yeah."

"Have you ever wanted to adopt a rabbit before?"

"I didn't know they existed until a decade ago," I point out. "And I've been kind of busy."

"Have you even had a pet before?" Ari adds. "You haven't in the time I've known you."

Okay, now I'm feeling ganged up on. "When I was younger I did, but it's not the easiest thing to look after a pet when you're a soldier—especially during times of crisis, which it was since before I met you."

"How long do rabbits usually live?" Caolan wonders, still typing into his phone.

This, I know. "As pets, eight to twelve years. Sometimes longer if they're thriving."

They all exchange glances again.

"Okay, what's going on? Why are you all being weird about this?"

Ari backs toward the security gate, and Hagen looks up at the ceiling, whistling, but Caolan's still smiling at me. "We're not being weird. I think it's sweet that you're willing to be a pet owner for a decade of your life so Elsking isn't lonely. I just hope you don't treat the new bunny like a second-class citizen."

Hagen's whistle cuts off, and he shoots Caolan a "what the fuck?" look.

I shake my head. "I wouldn't do that. If this bunny and I don't click tonight, I'll tell the rescue to find her another family."

The elevator doors open before Caolan can reply, and Candice steps out.

"We'll leave you to it," Hagen says. "Signal if you need help."

Because they'll be watching. Wonderful.

They exchange greetings with Candice as they pass her, and then she's stopping beside me with a warm smile.

"Did I hear something about trouble with the printer?"

CHAPTER TWENTY-SIX

Dáithí

I can't even remember the last time I had a workday off for no reason. I take vacation time, of course, but usually if I have a random day off, it's because I have an appointment or errand that can only be done on a weekday. A day off "just because" is different, and I can confirm that it's deliciously decadent.

My appointed spies for the day were Caolan and Candice, and they both reported several times that Eoin hadn't burned the place down and was keeping reasonably on top of things. That's honestly more than I expected—he's never worked as a receptionist before, our offices are busy, and we work with *dragons*. I made some calls yesterday to the worst trouble-makers in the office and threatened them with dire consequences if they weren't on their best behavior for the day. It wasn't for Eoin's benefit as much as to save me from having to deal with anything catastrophic tomorrow, though I'm not upset if Eoin benefitted from it. The job's enough of a challenge on its own without the extra zip dragons bring.

But office hours officially ended an hour ago, and the final report from Candice was that I can expect to find things in reasonable shape tomorrow. Eoin texted me not long after to say he needed to run an errand, but could he come over when he was done, so I'm expecting him soon, and looking forward to hearing how his day was. And not just because he was doing my job today.

The domesticity of my feelings toward Eoin scares the crap out of me.

Elsking and I are on the couch, watching an episode of *Dawson's Creek*, which Jared told me was formative to his teen years—and I can see why; it's incredibly addictive, even if all these supposed teenagers look ten years older than they should be—when I hear the key in the front door. I don't take my eyes off the screen, though. Is this the episode where Joey finally chooses between Pacey and Dawson?

"Dáithí?" Eoin calls—just as the credits roll. Damn it.

"In here," I reply, picking up the remote to stop the stream. As much as I desperately want to know what happens next, I'd rather spend the evening with Eoin.

Anyway, how long can this love triangle last? Aren't human teens supposed to be impulsive?

Eoin appears in the doorway, and the second his gaze lands on me, he smiles. "Hi."

"Hi." I scan him, my eyes skimming up and down his body. "You look unharmed."

His chuckle is natural but... nervous? Why's he nervous? "I need to apologize deeply for everything I've ever done to make your job harder, but before we get to that, I've got something to show you."

My brows shoot up. "I'm guessing this isn't a sexy show-and-tell."

"No." He shakes his head. "It's not bad, though. I did something that you could get mad about, and—"

"At work?" My hands freeze in Elsking's fur as my mind races with all the possibilities.

"Not at work. I promise, work was... well, not fine. You're a superhero for all the shit you put up with. But I didn't do anything bad at work, even though I want to buy the biggest hammer I can find and use it to smash the printer into pieces so small, we'll need a vacuum to clean them up."

I relax, laughter bubbling up inside me. "I'd offer to pay for the hammer, but it took me a long time to learn this printer's idiosyncrasies. Who knows what the next one will be like." I hold out a hand to him, not sure why he's still hovering in the doorway.

He doesn't seem to get the hint, staying right where he is. "I really hope I never have to learn. Anyway... I know it's going to seem like I'm being presumptuous, so I want to explain first that this is for me, too, and if you never want to see her again, that can happen."

"What? See who?" I'm so confused.

Taking a deep breath, he leans down to the side, out of my view, and when he straightens, he's holding... a pet carrier. I can't see inside it from this angle, but based on what he said a minute ago, I have a strong suspicion about what's inside.

"I think we might need more words now, Eoin."

He nods. "Yeah. Of course. I adopted a rabbit. She doesn't have a name yet, but she's four years old and her previous owner was an unscrupulous breeder. Human police removed her and a few others from his custody, and now they're being rehomed. I thought she and Elsking might like to be friends."

My heart aches thinking of how bad things must have been for law enforcement to get involved. "How many others?"

"I don't know, but Bobby at the shelter had a waitlist of people to call, so I think they're okay."

That's a relief, though it makes me wonder how Eoin managed to be ahead of those people. Does that mean he was on the list? "I bet Elsking would love to have a friend. I read online that rabbits prefer to have company."

The flash of guilt on Eoin's face answers all my questions, but he's coming into the room now, so I hold off on asking about it. He sets the carrier on the coffee table, and I sit up and lean forward, keeping Elsking in my arms just in case.

"She's very affectionate," Eoin's saying as he unlatches the door. "The vet report said that she's healthy, just under-weight, but we can fix that. She won't have to worry about not getting enough to eat or being forced to always stay preg-nant anymore." He reaches inside and withdraws her, and even though she's lovely, I can see immediately that she's too thin. Unlike Elsking, who's mostly white with one brown ear and brown patches around her eyes, this lady has golden brown fur all over—except for her belly, which is lighter. She's the color of a butterscotch candy, and from the way she cuddles close to Eoin, I'm willing to bet she's just as sweet.

"Aw, look at her," I gush, then pat the seat beside me. "Come over here, and let's introduce them."

Eoin joins me on the couch and sets the new bunny on his lap. She huddles close to him, and I can't tell if she's just shy or if this is trauma. "She's nervous," he says, worry entering his tone as he gives her gentle, reassuring pets. "It's okay, my sweet. Nobody will hurt you here."

My heart melts into a puddle. "Let her stay with you. Elsking will come there." If there's one thing I've learned about my bunny in the past couple of weeks, it's that she's curious about everyone and everything. I relax my hold on her, and within seconds, she's edging over toward Eoin's lap to check out the newcomer.

It's like watching her meet Jared's cat all over again, only without any concern about her being attacked. She sniffs around for a bit, getting progressively closer to the new bunny, then finally sniffs her directly. Goldie—which is *not* going to be her name, but will do for now—turns her head toward Elsking, and their little bunny noses touch.

Eoin and I make "cuteness overload" noises at the same time, and I grin at him. "I think they'll be fine."

"Ha. Yeah." He's watching the two rabbits in his very crowded lap with a little smile, and I decide to take advantage of his preoccupation.

"Did you get her because you were worried about Elsking being lonely?"

"Ye—" He cuts himself off and shoots me a guilty glance.

I wait him out, and eventually he sighs.

"Yes. I read a few articles about how rabbits are social and thrive when they're not alone, and then I spoke to a vet about it as well. It didn't seem right to not give Elsking and another rabbit every advantage. But I swear I'm not planning to just leave her with you. I have things for her at my place, and I'm her owner on all the paperwork." He eyes me, but I'm concentrating on keeping my expression blank. "I thought they could both go back and forth between our houses and keep each other company during the day while we're working."

I nod noncommittally, thoughts whirling, and turn my attention back to his lap, where Elsking has started grooming her new bestie. "Have you thought about names for her?"

Eoin's gaze is burning a hole in the side of my face, but I don't look up, and after a moment he says, "Not really. There was a woman at the shelter when I picked her up who suggested Goldie, but I don't love it."

I pull a face. "Me either. Though she is a gorgeous color. I know it's not very creative, but what about Butterscotch?"

The second the word leaves my mouth, she looks at me.

Eoin laughs delightedly. "Did you see that?"

"I did. Is that your name, then? Butterscotch?" I ask her, and her nose twitches. A smile takes over my lips.

"That's settled," Eoin announces. "My princess's name is Butterscotch." He strokes her ears, careful not to disturb either of them. "They seem to have made fast friends." It's not a question, but there's a tentative inquiry in his voice.

"I'm not mad, Eoin."

He sighs with relief.

"But we do need to talk."

"About the rabbits?"

"Yes, but not just that. Though, just so you know, you caring so much about the welfare of my pet makes me really fucking horny."

A strangled sound escapes his throat. "Good to know."

"And I agree, it would be best for them to keep each other company when we're working or out, and they can stay with us wherever we're staying at night. Were you planning this when you extended Elsking's hutch?"

He shrugs slightly. "Not exactly. I mostly wanted to give her some play tunnels, but the guy I ordered her new collar from mentioned that rabbits like company. I was still looking into it when I made the plan to extend the hutch, but I figured it couldn't hurt to make it big enough for two, just in case. I built the same one for my place, so it will feel familiar to them."

"That's so swee— Wait, what new collar?" He ordered a new collar for her?

"Oh. Well, you know how you weren't happy with the selection when you got her collar? I was looking online at what was available so I could send you some links, but nothing was good enough. So I contacted this company that makes them custom. I ordered one already, mostly to see if they do good work, and I figured if they do, you can design what you like for Elsking. And I'll get one for Butterscotch, too—they had fake yellow topazes that would look beautiful with her fur."

I bury my face in my hands, not sure whether to laugh or just break down. I thought I'd worked through all my conflicted feelings and come to a decision I was happy with, but I was so wrong.

"Dáithí? I'm sorry if I overstepped. I swear, I wasn't making decisions for you. I just didn't want you to spend time designing something and be disappointed if the quality turned out bad."

Shaking my head, I drop my hands and meet his worried gaze. "It's not that. I'm not mad, Eoin, and I'm so sorry you feel like you have to walk on eggshells around me."

"I don't," he says immediately, surprise dominating his expression. "If I did, I just wouldn't have done the things that might make you mad. But I also don't want to be pushy. Elsking's *yours*."

His insistence on respecting me—and the boundaries I've been setting—is all I needed for the last piece to click into place.

"We should call off the Summit of Love."

CHAPTER TWENTY-SEVEN

Eoin

DÁITHÍ'S WORDS hang between us. My eyes are locked on his face—is that fear? Determination?—while I try to process them. Is this... good? Bad? Does he want to call it off because he's made his decision or because he's realized it's pointless for me to try to prove something he doesn't want me to prove?

I was done worrying about the latter, but the fact that he actually called it the "Summit of Love," a name he's refused to use up until now, has shifted my worldview. Maybe I don't have as good a grip on this situation as I thought.

As the silence lengthens, his expression morphs more strongly into fear, and I pull myself together.

"You want to call it off?"

He nods, then clears his throat. "Yes."

"That's your call to make, if you want it." I choose my words carefully so I don't break down and beg—at least, not until I know for certain that this means the end of us. "Why? That is... why now? I thought I was doing well." I try not to hold my breath. It's counterproductive to thinking fast.

To my dismay, that seems to make him more unhappy.

"It's not that. You're... amazing, frankly. You've been excelling at every task, but the thing is, *you shouldn't have to.*" His voice cracks on the last words, and he stops to suck in air.

I don't know what to say. He's right; I shouldn't have to. I *don't* have to. This was my idea. I offered—insisted, in fact. There's no obligation for me to be here, completing tasks, and we both know it. But that's not what he means.

It's incredibly clear to me now that when Ari said he thought Dáithí had been hurt, I should have acted. I'd never force Dáithí to tell me something he didn't want to, but I could have let him know what I suspected and that I was ready to support him however he needed. Sometimes all people need is to know who's safe to talk to.

He's still staring at the floor, his jaw clenched, so I gather up the bunnies and stand slowly, then cross the room to settle them in the hutch, giving him a moment to settle his emotions. When I turn back, he's watching me with unmistakable longing... and regret.

My stomach sinks.

"Eoin," he whispers, but I seize my chance, returning to sit beside him. If distance makes it easier for him to end us, I'm not leaving his side the whole time he's speaking.

"You haven't forced me to do anything," I remind him gently, and he grimaces.

"That only makes it worse. Healthy relationships don't start like this, Eoin. We're both old enough to understand that—to know better. I never should have agreed to a challenge. You don't deserve to be tested when you haven't done anything to make me doubt you." He shakes his head. "You don't deserve to be tested at all. This was... wrong, and I'm sorry I put you through it."

I take a moment to consider what he's said and what he *hasn't*. I don't think he wants to break up, but guilt is clouding his judgment. "Why did you agree? If you'd stuck to your guns, we would have been over weeks ago."

"Yeah." He smiles sadly. "That's why I agreed. I didn't... I don't want us to be over, Eoin. I love you more than I've ever loved anyone in my life. More than I will ever love anyone else. If I think about waking up to a day where you're not in my life, it makes me not want to wake up that day."

Fear clutches me, but I ignore it. He's not in danger. "I'm here for all the days you want me to be."

Finally, he lifts his attention to me. "I'm so afraid."

"Of me?"

"No. Never. But yes." He pulls a face. "I'm doing this badly."

"You're fine. This has been worrying you."

"Yes. I tried to keep it from you, but that didn't work. So in the end, we both worried when I should have just..." He trails off with a restless gesture. "Some things aren't easy to talk about. Especially when telling you might hurt you. Especially when they're stupid and unjustified."

Now we're getting to the heart of things. "You're mad at yourself. I never thought the day would come where you said emotions were stupid," I tease, and miracle of miracles, I win a tiny smile.

"Neither did I," he admits. "But right now, it's so hard not to feel that way. I-I've said some unforgiveable things to you recently. You're an adult and you know your own mind and feelings. You know what you want from life. Questioning that and forcing you to prove something you should never have to prove when I should have just trusted you... that's unforgiveable, and I'm so sorry."

I wait a beat to make sure he's finished. "Don't you think I'm the one who gets to decide what I can forgive? Just like I'm the one who wanted the chance to prove myself. I appreciate the apology—deeply and sincerely, I do

—and I'm glad you agree that you should have trusted me, but I could have walked away then, and I didn't. I wanted to fight for us in the only way left to me, and I'm not sorry I did."

His eyes get wet, but before he can look away, I catch hold of his chin. "I love you, too, you know. So much that it's bursting from me. So much that I would happily do anything you needed of me. I'll say it again, Dáithí—I'm in your life for as long as you want me. If that means we face some hurdles while you work through your fears, I'm here for it."

A sob bursts from him, but the tears don't fall. "I'm afraid," he whispers. "I shouldn't be, but I am."

"'Should' isn't a word that applies to emotions," I tell him. "You're allowed to feel things, even if they're not logical. What scares you? What do you need from me?"

He lets out a shaky breath. "It pisses me off that you're being perfect right now and I'm... this." He waves at himself. "An emotional mess."

Startled, I cough to cover the laugh that wants to escape. "I'm not—actually, I'll take that. I'm perfect."

His elbow makes contact with my side, but not hard. "You're supposed to say I'm not a mess. The perfect score just went down."

This time I don't bother to hide my chuckle. "Baby, you're the most perfect person alive, including when you're a mess. I love your mess and your emotions. They're part of the whole package that's *you*."

The depth of love shining in his wet, wide eyes reassures me that we're going to be okay.

"When I was young, I trusted the wrong person, and he broke my heart," he blurts, then blows out a breath. I resist the impulse to demand who so I can race out to find the bastard and deliver him to Dáithí in chains. "It's not... The story isn't anything special. That's basically it. Logically, there's no reason for it to still be affecting my life thousands of years later."

"Logically, there's no reason for emotions at all," I point out. "But I wouldn't want to give mine up, even when they hurt. The dark moments make the sunshine ones so much sweeter."

He peers at me suspiciously. "You're thinking about that kids' movie, aren't you? The one where all the emotions are people living in human brains?"

"Maybe." It's lived rent-free in my head since I first watched it. Caolan suggested it after I complained that understanding how kids' brains work is too hard. Raðulfr visits with children a lot in his role as our leader, which means I have a lot of contact with them, too, but that never made it any easier. "The point is, I'm not judging you for still managing the aftereffects of something that hurt you deeply. Do you want to tell me the whole story? You don't have to."

"I know." He gives a little sigh, then leans against me, voluntarily touching me for the first time since this conversation began. "I think I want to, though."

A little more of the tension inside me eases. I put my arm around him and give him a little squeeze.

But as he speaks, the tension comes back. He's right that his story isn't anything uncommon, but that doesn't make what happened okay. He may have been an adult at the time, he may have willingly consented to the relationship and all it entailed—except being cheated on—but it's still clear to me that he was gaslighted by a predator. Alan saw something he wanted, was denied it, and then made it his mission to get it anyway on his own terms, whether Dáithí knew about those terms or not. Worse, though, is that when he didn't want it anymore, he went out of his way to do as much harm as he could.

I wait until he's finished. "May I hold you?"

The words are barely out of my mouth before he's crawling halfway into my lap, my arms closing around him instinctively as he lays his head on my shoulder. "I'm sorry," he mumbles, but I just give him a squeeze.

"There's nothing to be sorry about, baby. I'm... I ache for the pain and insecurity you've been carrying all this time, but I can't say I'm not a little relieved too."

He lifts his head, his face now so close to mine. "Relieved?"

"That your hesitation isn't about me. It's not that you don't want to commit to *me*."

"No, but also... I didn't trust that you weren't like him." His lips tremble, but he firms them almost immediately.

"That's true," and it stings, I can't lie. "You acted based on past experience. That's completely understandable—we all do it. Even at work, it's standard in most industries to base plans on past results. It's how you respond to live results that matters, and Dáithí, you're apologizing to me right now and calling off the Summit of Love because you know you were wrong. That's what's most important."

He puts his head back down. "I *was* wrong. I just wish I hadn't had to put you through all this to admit it."

Kissing his hair, I ask, "Are you still scared?"

His silence tells me what I need to know.

"It's okay if you are, baby. I am too, a little."

"You are?" It's barely a whisper, and I lean my head against his.

"Yeah. There are a lot of ways either or both of us can fuck things up, or that life can. We've been through enough to know nothing comes with a guarantee, and it terrifies me that something might happen to you."

Dáithí's hand creeps up my body and cups my cheek. "But you want to do this—us—anyway?"

"More than anything."

We sit for a moment, both breathing shakily.

"Me too."

The weakness that overtakes me proves I wasn't as sure of him as I thought I was, but that doesn't matter now. I lift my head, and when he straightens to look at me, I study his face. It's tear-streaked and flushed, but the determination and love in his eyes are balm to my soul.

"I can call you my boyfriend now?" I check.

He nods and leans forward to kiss me. "Boyfriend, partner, significant other... whatever will tell the world that we belong to each other."

The grin that breaks out on my face is so wide, it hurts.

CHAPTER TWENTY-EIGHT

Dáithí

EOIN's blatant joy prompts pangs of guilt, but I shove them aside. He's forgiven me, and even if I never quite manage to forgive myself for what I've done to him, I won't let him know. It would just make him feel bad.

We stay wrapped up in each other for a little while longer, kissing and just enjoying being together. It feels different now, without the emotional distance I put between us. I'd hoped the barrier would keep me from being hurt when things ended, but it never worked that way. I still fell hard for Eoin —the only thing it did was prevent us from being completely happy. That's done now.

But if kissing Eoin feels more intense and meaningful now that I'm not trying to protect myself, what's sex going to be like?

No time like the present to find out.

I break away from his mouth, then change my mind and go back for another nibble. He tastes better than anything, ever. But... "Get naked."

"Huh?" He blinks at me, eyes a little dazed from all the

kissing, and triumph fizzles through me. I do that to him—this powerful, respected man. I reduce him to dazed lust.

"Naked," I repeat. "I want to fuck my boyfriend." I untangle myself from his arms, stand, grab the hem of my T-shirt, and pull it off over my head. Eoin scrambles to his feet with gratifying speed, and by the time I've dropped my pants, he's nearly caught up.

And then he drops to his knees. It's a beautiful sight, this strong, powerful man kneeling for me, and my heart clutches in my chest.

"Kneel up on the couch," he orders, and I frown, trying to work out those logistics. He's tall, but not that tall. "Facing the back."

Facing the... oh. *Ohhhhh*. I turn around so fast, I nearly fall over, then scramble onto the couch and present my ass. For a moment, nothing happens, and I swear I tremble with anticipation.

Eoin's breath wafts across my most sensitive skin, and my eyes drift closed—only to open when he trails a finger slowly down my cleft.

"You're going to torture me, aren't you?"

His chuckle is his only reply as his finger teases my hole... and then it's replaced by the wet heat of his tongue, and I forget everything I was thinking.

He's so... damn... good... at this.

Soon the nerve-tingling pleasure morphs into driving need, his talented attention winding me up into nonsensical babble as I push back into his mouth. My hand slides down to grab my cock, squeezing around the base before I pump it once. Too dry... What's the lube spell? I can't *think*.

Then Eoin's mouth is gone, and I whimper at the loss, but it's replaced within seconds by the nudge of his hard dick.

"Yesss," I gasp, pushing out eagerly—not that my muscles have any tension left in them. He slides in even more easily than an eternity of sloppy rimming should allow, and when his hand comes around to take over working my cock, it's wet with lube. Obviously he's still capable of remembering the spell.

I'll have to see what I can do to change that.

Bracing my forearms on the back of the couch, I flex my hips, forcing him all the way into me, and his choked gasp is my reward.

"Easy," he breathes. "You'll hurt—"

"I won't. Come on, Eoin. Do me hard. I want to feel like your cock is permanently embedded in me." Remembering my own drunken rambling from the night at the club, I add, "Merge me with the universe." I punctuate it by clenching my ass muscles around him.

The sound he makes is part laugh and part groan, but he takes me at my word, pulling back and ramming into me just the way I want it. I thrust my ass backward to meet him, and he doesn't even need to jack me off—the tight clasp of his hand and the friction from our movements is going to do the work for him.

I try to focus on making this as good for him as possible. On this first time with us being official boyfriends being special, noteworthy. I have no idea if I hold up my end, but I know I'll never forget this.

"Fuck, Dáithí, I'm going to come," he grunts. "Are you close? Please?"

"Come, baby. I love you."

The low-pitched scream sounds like it's torn from his throat as his thrusts stutter, and the liquid heat of his cum floods me. That's all it takes to send me into the best orgasm of my life.

MUCH LATER, in bed, I cuddle up to Eoin's side, secure and warm. Maybe I still can't know what the future holds. Eoin would never deliberately hurt me, but that doesn't mean his feelings won't one day change, and if that happens, it will shatter me. But I don't need to let fear of something that might never come keep me from basking in his love now.

Even if that means living with the tiny spark of doubt I can't quite shake.

I trust Eoin, and I trust that one day, that doubt will be buried under all the love he's given me.

"Dáithí?" he asks, his voice cutting through the darkness.

"Hm?" I thought he was asleep already.

"I don't want you to think I don't understand how hard it was for you to give me your trust. I don't want you to think I don't appreciate the commitment you made to me tonight."

My heartbeat drums loudly in my ears. "W-Why would I think that?"

"Because I'm going to finish the Summit of Love."

WE'RE STILL ARGUING about it when we get off the elevator at work the next morning. Eoin refuses to see reason.

"It's not necessary," I insist for the millionth time. "I don't want you to."

"Uh-huh. I'm still going to, though."

I stomp over to my desk, unlock the ward on the bottom drawer, and grab my spray bottle.

"So that's where you put it," he says from right behind me. Good. Saves me having to walk back to him. I straighten and aim the nozzle at him as I squeeze the handle.

"Hey!" He takes two big steps back, but I follow, spraying again and again. "Stop that! Dáithí!" There's an edge of laughter in his voice, and I spray him again. He's getting pretty damp.

"What's this?"

I glance over at where the king and Brandt have just gotten off the elevator. It's not the ideal moment for both my bosses to walk in, but I've never hidden my habit of using unconventional tactics. I even sprayed Brandt once.

"My boyfriend is being a stubborn, unreasonable ass, so I'm correcting his behavior." I follow Eoin as he continues backing away from me.

"It's not going to work," he insists, and I spritz again. Lucky I refilled not that long ago.

"Make sure you mop up before anyone slips," the king says mildly, and I cackle at Eoin's betrayed expression.

"Sir!"

"Boyfriend?" Brandt demands. "I thought Dáithí didn't use that word."

"He does now." Eoin's grin is huge. "We're official."

Aw. I love seeing how happy that makes him. *Spritz, spritz.* His yelp is deeply rewarding.

"Congratulations!" Brandt whips out his phone and... yep, he starts recording. "Is this your first argument as an official couple?"

"Yes," Eoin says, lunging toward me in an attempt to grab the bottle. I dance out of his reach.

"It's not an argument," I contradict. "That would require us both to be using reason and logic, which he is *not*." I dart closer and spray him before scrambling back again.

"Well, now I'm curious," His Majesty declares, just as the elevator doors open and a group of our coworkers exit—then stop and stare. The king waves them on, and they reluctantly go, dragging their feet and looking over their shoulders. Gossip is currency around here, and news is going to spread fast.

I don't care.

"We're official now," I repeat what Eoin already told them, chasing him around my desk, "but this stubborn fool claims he's still going to continue with the stupid challenges." I refuse to call it the Summit of Love again. Not in public. It's bad enough that Eoin heard me say it out loud.

"Why?" Brandt asks. "Speak up, please." He's still pointing his phone camera at us.

"Because he's a fool." I spritz to punctuate the sentence, even though Eoin's not close enough to get the benefit of it. It makes me feel better. Maybe I should get the other bottle —the itching one.

"A fool in love, maybe," he counters, and our bosses both say, "Aww."

"I'm glad you're recording," the king adds. "Jared will want to see this."

"You're not helping, sir," Eoin calls.

"I'm not trying to. After all, you weren't helpful when Jared and I were first dating."

It's true, but the urge to defend Eoin rises strongly in me. "He was looking out for—Hey!" My boyfriend took advantage of my distraction to get close enough to steal the bottle —while I was defending him!

"You can have this back when I go," he tells me, and I narrow my eyes.

"Excuse me?"

"Run, Eoin," Brandt suggests, still filming. I ignore him, focusing on my *boyfriend*.

"I'm not going to let you squirt water at me when I haven't done anything wrong," my aforementioned boyfriend asserts. "But I will help you mop up the water."

I fold my arms across my chest. "Why are you doing this?"

Confused, he glances at the floor. "Because it's wet and we don't want anyone to slip."

"No! Not that. This!" I gesture wildly.

Eoin grins, his arms loosely at his sides with my spray bottle dangling from one hand. I eye it and wonder what the chances are of me being able to snatch it back and hit him over the head with it.

"Use more words, Dáithí. 'This' is pretty broad."

The elevator doors open again just in time for everyone inside to hear me shout, "Your asinine insistence on completing the Summit of Love!"

There's a sudden, blanketing silence, and then someone inside the elevator says, "Hurry, hit the Door Close button."

I squeeze my eyes shut, heat flooding my cheeks as someone else says, "No! I want to hear. Let me off!"

There's a jumble of voices, and then I open my eyes to see a few people getting out of the elevator while behind them, a woman stabs repeatedly at the control panel—probably the Door Close button.

"Good morning," the king says to the newcomers. "I'm sure you're eager to get to your desks." It's a thinly veiled order, but from the way all three drag their feet, none of them is eager to leave. His Majesty keeps an expectant look on them all the way to the security gate, but the second he turns away, a blond elf from Accounting speaks up.

"What's the Summit of Love? Is that a sex thing? If it's a sex thing, I'd like to know about it."

"It's not a sex thing," Brandt says, and her face falls in disappointment. "It's a love thing."

She opens her mouth, but the king clears his throat, and she changes her mind, following the others through the security gate instead.

I turn my glare on Eoin. "Thanks for that. Becoming a laughingstock has always been high on my to-do list."

"Anybody who dares to laugh at you will regret it," he informs me, then shocks me by handing the spray bottle to

Brandt, who gasps and studies it like it's both radioactive and the meaning of life. I'm still sputtering when Eoin catches me loosely in his arms, leaving just enough space between us so we can see each other's faces.

"I love you," he says solemnly. "What you did last night means more to me than any other gift I've ever been given. You love me, you trust me, and you're committing to me, openly and publicly. I know how hard that is for you, and that just makes it mean more."

"Then—"

"Uh-uh." He shakes his head. "Let me finish. It's because of how much it means and how hard it is that I want to finish the challenges. Do you remember the night I said I wanted to do this?"

I'll never forget. "Yes."

"Do you remember telling me I didn't have to, and why I said I wanted to?" He doesn't wait for me to answer. "I want to prove beyond any shadow of doubt that you've made the right decision, so that one day in the future, when we have a stupid fight or I forget something that's important to you or whatever might happen that causes doubt to rear its ugly head in your brain, you can remember the Summit of Love and shove all those fears aside."

My breath catches. How can he know me this well? Know what I barely know about myself? "Eoin..." It's barely a whisper, and I can't quite manage to put my feelings into words.

He leans in and kisses me, murmuring, "I know," against my lips.

Whoever said the perfect man didn't exist was wrong. He does... and he's mine.

EPILOGUE

Eoin

EARLY OCTOBER

IF YOU'D ASKED me a year ago how many times I'd sit at my boss's dining table while a bunch of coworkers and friends discussed my romantic life at my request, I'd have said zero. And yet, somehow this is the second time this year.

Hopefully it'll be the last ever.

Still, I'm strangely glad to be here. Everyone's still finding their seats and talking loudly, and they're about to ask me and Dáithí a lot of personal questions, but there's something about knowing they're here because they want us to be happy together that makes me feel good.

Well... all of them except Steffen are here because they want us to be happy. He's here because Brandt made him come—he told me so. It's nice to have him here anyway.

"I wish I had my spray bottle," Dáithí mutters from the seat beside me, but he's smiling at the chaos, and I reach over and lace my fingers with his before resting both our hands on the tabletop. Then we wait.

And wait.

For fuck's sake, how long does it take to sit in a chair and shut up?

Eventually, they're all sitting, and more or less quiet, so Dáithí clears his throat. "I'd thank you all for coming, but if it were up to me, none of us would be here." Even though he appreciates the reasons I'm doing this and sometimes looks at me with heart eyes because of it, there's still a lot of grudging disgruntlement in his voice.

It makes me smile.

"Anyway, Eoin has completed all the tasks on the list, including the redacted ones, so it's time to end this once and for all." He sits back, still holding my hand, while I bask smugly in the knowledge that I managed to complete tasks without even knowing what they were. That's a special skill.

Caolan stands, smiling beatifically. "If you'll all turn your attention to the wall," he gestures toward the end of the table and the expanse of wall above the sideboard, from where a painting has been temporarily relocated. This time, he was determined to be able to show us all his presentation, so he brought a projector with him. Even as we obediently look, he casts a spell to darken the area around the wall and allow the projection to be seen clearly.

"Oooh," Alistair murmurs appreciatively. "That's so much cooler than turning the lights off."

"Before we discuss Eoin's performance—"

Snickers and a round of jeers break out, because apparently we're all just that mature. I smirk. "I'm very proud of my performance, thanks."

"Me too," Dáithí says loyally, then winks at me. "Especially—"

"Dude," Hagen interrupts. "No. I'm still recovering from all the things I heard when I was his roommate. I don't need any more trauma to recover from."

I laugh, because he's the roommate that caused the

trauma. Things were a lot less sticky in the house after he moved out.

"I'm not sure I should be here for this conversation," Raðulfr says. "This probably falls into the category of things I shouldn't know about the people who work for me."

"That's the category that has all the good stuff in it," Brandt objects. "We definitely need to be here for this conversation."

"*Anyway*," Caolan says loudly, "before we move on, I'm going to recap the tasks involved in the Summit of Love."

Dáithí groans at the mention of the name, but I know he's a tiny bit fond of it, deep down inside. Waaaay deep down. Even if he refuses to say it out loud unless he absolutely has to.

Caolan clicks the thing in his hand that looks like a very boring dildo but isn't, and the image on the wall changes to a bulleted list. "Plan and execute a series of dates," he reads. "This was later agreed to be three. Take a shift at Dáithí's job. Clean Dáithí's apartment. Surprise Dáithí." He pauses, then clicks his dildo again. The image changes to show the heading "Redacted Tasks" with nothing beneath it.

I bet he's trying to build anticipation. Caolan's always been the dramatic type, in an earnest, understated way. According to rumor, the first time he met his boyfriend, he made a flowery, over-the-top speech about David's perfection. It's only gotten worse since he fell in with his new friends.

"And finally," he declares, voice thrumming with drama, "we can reveal to Eoin the redacted tasks."

I lean forward. Maybe he's being over the top, but I can't deny I'm eager to know what they are. After I told Dáithí I was going to finish the challenge, he refused to tell me on principle, even though according to him it didn't matter if I knew because he was choosing me anyway. I love it when he's mean.

Click.

The first item of a bulleted list appears on the wall. *Look after a dependent living entity.*

I frown, then when the pieces come together, hiss at Dáithí, "Did you adopt Elsking to test me?"

"No, but this task was the prompt that reminded me how much I wanted another pet. I wouldn't have adopted her otherwise."

If I didn't know him so well and hadn't seen how much he adores her, I'd have serious doubts. "What—"

"Could we hold all discussion, please?" Alistair interrupts. "We'll address each task in turn, but it's important we keep to the agenda."

Maybe Dáithí was right and we should have called the whole thing off a month ago.

Caolan clicks again, and another bullet point appears. *Be responsible for something important to Dáithí.*

Yikes. I don't think I've done that. Keeping my face expressionless, I try to catch Ari's eye, maybe get a hint about what this task actually means, but he's glaring at the tabletop. He's been in a rotten mood since the Community Hockey League training camp a few weeks back. Longer, actually— since he went to apologize to Felix Ansas. It probably doesn't help that the king and Jared decided they wanted to set up an outreach collaboration between the DEA and the Warhammers to get young elves and dragons involved in the sport, and Ari got assigned as liaison until someone else can take over. Technically, it's a job that falls outside the scope of the security team, but since they wanted to get it started immediately to coincide with the season, nobody from the PR department or Caolan's projects team was available to spearhead it. Jared suggested that Ari temporarily step into the role, with support from PR, until workloads could be reshuffled... and neither Ari nor I could think of a reason to refuse.

Admittedly, I didn't try very hard. Dáithí asked me not to. I'm not sure what that's about, but I hope to find out soon.

The dildo clicks again, and the heading changes to The Dates, a table appearing below. It's divided into three columns, each containing a bulleted list. Caolan must really like those. The lists are headed Baseball, Club, and Hiking.

"Let's begin with the first date," Caolan says as I read the points in each list. "I've included the top-level feedback you all provided, but this is our chance to discuss it in detail."

"Or we could *not* discuss it in detail," Dáithí counters.

"Yes!" Noah slaps a hand on the table. "That. I like that idea."

"But—"

"No."

"What if we just raise any concerns?" Alistair suggests. "Don't steal all our joy, please."

Noah's face says pretty clearly that he'd happily take the job of joy stealer, but he just sighs. "We're spending five minutes on each task. I'll be generous and give you six minutes for this first one, so you can divide them evenly between the three dates."

Team Bro jaws collectively drop, and Alistair starts sputtering.

"I'll time them," Steffen announces, pulling out his phone.

Dáithí edges his chair closer to mine and leans against me. "This is more fun than I thought it would be," he whispers.

Caolan, Andrew, and Alistair try to argue with Steffen, but he simply taps his phone screen and says, "Your time has begun."

"Baseball!" Hagen shouts wildly. "Eoin gets points for picking an activity Dáithí likes, cranking it up a level to fancy, and... and..."

"Not just fancy," Jared points out. "The fancy part was a bonus. He thought about how much Dáithí likes gossip and managed to find a way to combine two activities into a super-date."

I preen. Super-date? I'll take it.

Niamh's nodding. "Yeah. Dáithí got to dress up, and he didn't just hear gossip, he got to hang out with people and make new friends. He likes all those things."

"Any negatives?" Andrew asks, and when nobody speaks up, he nods. "Next date... the nightclub."

"Does it count?" Brandt asks, and when a round of gasps goes up, he holds up his hands. "I'm not saying it doesn't, but we need a clear ruling on this. It was a group activity. Does it count as a date?"

I... didn't think of that. Dáithí likes hanging out with friends, and he especially likes clubbing with people he knows. I didn't consider whether that would disquali—

"It counts," he says firmly, and I exhale with enough force to make my shoulders slump.

Brandt grins wickedly. "Great! I wasn't invited, but it sounds like it was a fun night."

Oh, fuck. "I—"

"Ignore him," the king instructs. "We don't have time for this."

The reminder that Steffen is timing us sends Team Bro into a flurry of discussion.

"Dáithí loves dancing—"

"Clubbing in general, really—"

"—and the VIP area with bottle service elevated it—"

"—got to dress up again—"

"—arranged for his favorite DJ to be there—"

"—hanging out with friends—"

"What? Stop," Dáithí cuts in. "What did you just say? About my favorite DJ?"

"She was the featured DJ that night," Alistair explains.

"Adjoa K. She's your favorite, right?" He looks around. "I'm sure someone said that."

Dáithí gestures impatiently, and I worry my lower lip with my teeth. There's a very slim chance this isn't going to go my way.

"She is, but what did you mean, Eoin arranged for her to be there?"

All eyes turn to me, and I shrug awkwardly. "She's your favorite."

He gapes. "You... *how*? I *knew* she wasn't supposed to be in town! How did you do this?"

"It's better if we don't talk about that." Ethically, I'm not supposed to use my position at the DEA for personal benefit. I don't think the king or Brandt—especially Brandt—will care in this case, but some of the calls I made to arrange it were to professional contacts, not personal ones, even though I made it clear the event wasn't DEA sponsored and paid for it myself.

Dáithí gives me the heart eyes I love so much. "You did all that just so I could have my favorite DJ?"

"I'd do anything within my power for you."

A chorus of "Aww" goes around the table, everyone smiling fatuously.

Then Hagen shouts, "Time!" and the conversation restarts.

"Any negatives from the club?" Caolan demands, barely pausing for a response before continuing, "Date three: the hike."

"It wasn't just a hike," Brayan reminds them. "There was an overnight stay in a cabin too."

Noah perks up. "Yeah, about that. Why didn't you just camp? Camping under the stars in the middle of nature... I thought you elves would love that."

"I'm off camping at the moment," Dáithí replies. "Eoin

did the exact right thing by finding an off-grid cabin for us instead."

"Not much difference between off-grid and camping, especially when it's just for one night," Jared muses, but Dáithí doesn't offer more information, and Jared's too polite to pry.

There's a short discussion about the good points of the date, but I lose some metaphorical points because Dáithí didn't like being away from Elsking and also missed an episode of a show he's been watching. Personally, I think that last one doesn't count because the show's on a streaming service and he watched it when we got home, but Brandt insisted the timing was important.

Caolan looks to Dáithí. "Task one: pass or fail?"

"Pass."

A cheer goes up. If I wasn't basking in victory, I might think our friends and colleagues are way too invested in this. Ari even puts aside his sulk to grin at me.

The celebration is cut short when Steffen announces, "I've reset the timer."

"You make it very hard to like you," Andrew tells him, and gets a blank look in response.

"Why do you think I want you to like me?"

Brandt sighs, but the rest of us, especially those who've known Steffen a long time, stifle laughter. I don't care if he doesn't want to be my friend—he's a solid colleague and a good man. His quirks are his business, including his identical twin brother who tried to steal his identity a few years back.

"Next task," Alistair says. "Caolan?"

Click goes the dildo, and the next bulleted list appears. "I think we can all agree that Eoin's shift as a receptionist was… unique."

Noah smirks. "Entertaining, you mean. I saw the security footage and heard the stories."

"I did my best," I defend, then turn to Dáithí. "Did I fuck it up too badly?"

He shakes his head. "You didn't fuck it up at all. I'd never normally leave someone who doesn't have experience in the job alone to manage things like that on their first day, but you coped fine."

Traces of guilt force me to admit, "I ignored the phones a few times."

My boyfriend shrugs. "So? I do that sometimes too, if I've got a lot of people waiting. You didn't yell at any visitors, didn't mess up the booking system, didn't accidentally take the whole phone system down, didn't destroy the printer... and there wasn't a huge backlog of work waiting for me when I got in the next day. You even left the desk clean and tidy. As far as I'm concerned, this task is a pass."

"Hey!" Hagen snaps. "Don't you want our feedback?"

Dáithí raises a brow, and Alistair rushes to speak before the whole presentation can be derailed.

"We agree that Eoin did well on this, but we want to highlight a few areas in particular."

"Like?"

"Well, have you noticed that people are getting better at following the protocol for visitors and meeting rooms?"

Frowning, Dáithí nods. "Actually, yes. I only have to follow up with a couple now, and they're always... apologetic."

"There are still people disregarding the security policies for visitors?" Steffen demands, looking up from his phone. "Who?"

Andrew makes a sweeping gesture. "Eoin brought in reinforcements."

"He..." Dáithí turns to me. "You told on everyone to Steffen?"

I wince. Was that cheating? Should I have handled it myself? "Maybe?"

He dissolves into laughter. "I wish I'd thought of that!"

"So you're not mad?" I check.

He shakes his head. "No, of course not. You got the job done and in the process made it easier for me to do. I'm grateful." Leaning in, he steals a kiss, then looks at Alistair. "Can I call it a pass now?"

"Wait," Ari demands. "We need to deduct points for Eoin almost punching the delivery guy."

"*What?*" Dáithí shoots upright, his hand sliding out of mine.

I glare at my second-in-command. "I didn't almost punch him!"

He smirks, getting his revenge for the hockey assignment. "That's right, you were going to rip his arms off instead."

"Someone tell me what happened, right *now*," Dáithí demands.

"I would also be interested to hear this," Raðulfr adds, glancing at Brandt. "Did you know about it?"

"Pfft." Brandt waves a hand as though possible assault isn't even worth mentioning. "Hagen mentioned it. They got there in time to make Eoin remember he's sensible, and nothing happened." He pauses, then adds, "I would have at least put a little itching spell on him."

It's probably not a good thing when I agree with a dragon's illogical and borderline illegal idea.

"It's not my proudest moment," I say in an attempt to smooth things over. "The delivery guy made it pretty clear that he's been hitting on Dáithí, and I... got... jealous. I wouldn't have actually hurt him." I'm pretty sure.

"Frankie?" Dáithí looks astounded. "You got jealous of *Frankie?*"

It's only the fact that he obviously thinks that's ridiculous that stops me from spiraling over him immediately knowing which delivery guy I'm talking about.

"Your friend Frankie told Eoin he thought he had a shot with you," Hagen says gleefully. *Why are we friends, again?* "Eoin was ready to use some hardcore magic on him before we arrived to distract him."

Dáithí gives a disbelieving little laugh. "You were going to... on *Frankie*... because he thinks he has a shot with me?"

I shrug uncomfortably. "I didn't say it was reasonable. And I wouldn't have done it," I repeat, because that part's important.

"He's a child still—even for a human, he's barely an adult. How could you give his little crush enough weight to be jealous over it? He never had a shot with me."

"I know." It comes out on a sigh. "But some days, it felt like I didn't either."

His expression softens, a trace of his old guilt mixed in with the love there. I can't take that guilt away, but I hope it fades as our life together continues. "Eoin, you stood me up on our first date and stuck me with the check, and I still agreed to go out with you again. Even when I was trying to protect my heart, I couldn't make myself let you go. Trust me... you have all the shots and never need to be jealous."

"Aw," Andrew says, then elbows Noah. "How come you never talk to me like that?"

Noah rolls his eyes. "Because you'd take it the wrong way."

"Time!"

I blink toward Steffen, who hasn't lost sight of his goal while the rest of us bickered. He narrows his eyes on Caolan. "Next task."

Caolan doesn't look happy, but he nods. "Dáithí already said this was a pass. Unless he's changed his mind?"

"Nope."

"Then let's move on. Cleaning Dáithí's apartment." The dildo clicks, and he shoots me an approving look. "The scent spell was very clever. I'm borrowing that idea to impress David."

Andrew laughs. "You're going to make your place smell like itemized lists and excellent timekeeping?"

Caolan's smug smile suggests there are a few other things David likes the smell of.

"This task is a pass too," Dáithí says, and Alistair groans.

"You're taking all the fun out of this."

"I don't know what you want me to say. The place was cleaner than I've ever gotten it, smells amazing, and is more organized. And he improved Elsking's hutch. We should probably combine the discussion of this task with the living entity one, because the hutch extension covers both."

"If it means we finish faster, yes. Please," Noah begs.

"Hold on." Jared half raises a hand. "Before we talk about the hutch, I want to know if Eoin used spells to clean."

"He was allowed to," Niamh defends before I can open my mouth.

"Yeah, I know. I'm not saying it's a bad thing. I just want all the details."

Faces turn toward me.

"No. I didn't know the exact spells I wanted, and it would have taken longer to design and fine-tune some than it did to just clean manually," I explain.

"Damn," Jared mutters. "Guess I can't throw out the mop yet."

"Let's stay focused," Caolan says with a worried glance toward Steffen, who's watching his phone intently. "Eoin not only improved Elsking's living conditions, he did research on rabbits and adopted one that had been mistreated so they could both be happier. Thoughts?"

"Don't forget the custom collars," Ari chimes in. "The whole team wondered if he had kinks."

Dáithí laughs so hard, he has to grab the table for

support. Across from me, the king raises a brow. "The whole team? This is one of those things happening in the office that I'm better off not knowing about, isn't it?"

I cringe. "They only jumped to that conclusion because they have dirty minds. The site I was looking at is specifically for pet products."

That just makes Dáithí laugh harder, and I can't help smiling. When he finally subsides, he adds, "Even before he did all that, Eoin was looking out for Elsking—and he did it without knowing it was one of the challenges. This task is a pass too."

A round of applause breaks out.

"What's next?" Hagen asks. "Taking care of something important to Dáithí, right?"

Nerves try to take over my stomach, and I concentrate on breathing evenly. We wouldn't be here if I hadn't at least somewhat met the criteria for this task. I just wish I knew—

"This one's easy," Dáithí says confidently. "He's been doing it all along—when he was so careful not to mess things up on reception, when he didn't reorganize my house the way he would have it, when he extended Elsking's hutch, when he put my feelings ahead of everything else. He takes care of everything he thinks might be important to me, and he always has. Including my heart."

My love for him is so overwhelming in that moment, I can barely breathe. Every word he said is true, but I don't do it because I'm trying to curry favor. It's just that what's important to him is important to me—*he's* important to me. But I can't find the words for that, so instead I haul his chair right up beside mine and kiss him until he's just at breathless—

"Time!"

Dáithí's mouth trembles with suppressed laughter under

mine, and my lips curve in a smile to match. We might have been swept away by the moment, but Steffen wasn't.

Breaking our kiss, I push my chair back a little and pull Dáithí into my lap. He gives me a stern look but allows it, relaxing back against me.

"We'll mark that as a pass," Alistair declares, grinning sappily. "I love romance."

"Last one, then." Caolan clicks his dildo, and I wonder who signed off on the design of it. They had to realize what it looked like, right? "Surprise Dáithí."

"That was the clubbing date," Brayan says, but Brandt frowns.

"I thought it was the hutch extension?"

"Wait," Noah cuts in. "Are we allowed to count those for two tasks?"

Hagen folds his arms. "Dáithí?"

"You guys wrote the rules. It never said anywhere that any of the other challenges had to be a surprise for me, so I've been counting every surprise since we started this toward this task."

"Really?" That surprises *me*. He's been counting all of them?

"Sure." He starts ticking off on his fingers. "The suite at the baseball, Adjoa K., the scent spell and Elsking's hutch, Butterscotch... they were all surprises that made me happy. And then when I told you I wanted to call the challenges off and just be happy together, you surprised me again by insisting on completing them all. You knew what I needed better than I did, and that was the point of this task."

"That's not why—" He puts his hand over my mouth.

"I know. But that just makes it mean more." He glances around the table. "He passed this one too."

The cheers that break out this time put the earlier ones to shame, and Dáithí and I grin foolishly at each other.

"Just checking," Alistair shouts over the noise, "this means you're staying together as boyfriends?"

In the blink of an eye, Dáithí's grin turns to a scowl, and he aims it at the big hellhound. "We already were. I told you, if it was up to me, we would have called this off a month ago."

"So we're done, then!" Noah jumps to his feet. "I'm happy for you both, blah blah. Let's go, Andrew."

Steffen's already hovering beside Brandt's chair, but the wingleader doesn't seem to be in any rush. As everyone begins to rise and gather their things, talking loudly, I kiss the side of Dáithí's neck.

"Hi, boyfriend."

His body shakes with his chuckle. "You're ridiculous." But his eyes are soft with affection as he stands and pulls me to my feet. "Let's go home."

We manage two steps before Raðulfr and Jared stop us.

"Congratulations," Jared says, hugging Dáithí. "It's good to see you this happy." He offers me his hand to shake. "We didn't start off right, but it's hard to hate you when I see how much you love my friend."

I clear my throat, stupidly touched. "Thank you. I'm sorry for—"

He shakes his head. "No apology needed. I understand your actions—I did even then."

It's not hard to read between his words. He understands why I did what I did, but that doesn't mean he didn't dislike me for it—I had to earn more than that.

Raðulfr clears his throat. "We'll let you sneak out in a moment, but before you go, I just wanted to ask if there's anything you want me to tell you."

Huh? He's not usually this cryptic. Is he hinting that we should ask for a day off work or something?

"You mean do we want to know if we're paired souls?"

Dáithí asks, and my jaw drops. Fuck! I hadn't even thought of that, because—

"Yes," Raðulfr says.

Dáithí looks at me. "What do you think?"

"This could be an extra assurance for you." It could also go the other way, which would be a disaster for me.

"You're right." He turns back to the king and Jared. "Thank you, but I don't need to know. I love Eoin, and whatever the future might hold in store for us isn't important to who we are now." He smiles up at me. "I don't mind if you want to know, though. I can wait over there."

It takes me a moment to speak, because I'm choking on the emotions his words caused. "I don't need to know." My voice is hoarse. "All I need is you."

Forever.

Thanks for reading *Enticing the Elf*! I hope you loved Eoin and Dáithí's story. Ari and Felix will get their HEA in *Falling for the Felid*. Look for them in 2026.
If you haven't read Jared and Raðulfr's story yet, check out
Wooing the Wiccan.

Want to try something different from me? *Couture* is next - a contemporary MM romance between a fashion stylist and a designer.

We talk spoilers in my Facebook reader group, RoMMance with Becca & Louisa.
Or you can subscribe to my newsletter to get all updates and access to bonus scenes: https://bit.ly/LouisaMBonus.

For early access to chapters of my upcoming books, artwork, and other bonus material, check out my Patreon here: patreon.com/louisamasters

ALSO BY LOUISA MASTERS

Saddles & Suits

Alistair's Extraordinaries

Grave Situation

Elemental Men: The Complete Series

Style Me

Rebrand

Couture

Elf Magic

Wooing the Wiccan

Enticing the Elf

The Collective

Higher Demon

Demon Hunter

Demons-In-Law

Asher

Micah

Zachary

Franklin U

Mr. Romance

The Holigay Hookup *related novella

Batting Style

Ghostly Guardians

Spirited Situation

Vortex Conundrum

Conduit Crisis

Gateway Catastrophe

Here Be Dragons

Dragon Ever After

The Professor's Dragon

The Dragon Experiment

Conspiracy of Dragons

Hidden Species

Demons Do It Better

One Bite With A Vampire

Hijinks With A Hellhound

Sorcerers Always Satisfy

Hidden Species Box Set

Met His Match

Charming Him

Offside Rules

A Christmas Chance (novella)

Between the Covers (M/F)

Joy Universe

I've Got This

Follow My Lead

In Your Hands

Take Us There

Novellas

Fake It 'Til You Make It (permafree)

One Golden Night

O Hell, All Ye Shoppers

Out of the Office

After the Blaze

Blokes Down Under Novella Collection

ABOUT THE AUTHOR

Louisa Masters started reading romance much earlier than her mother thought she should. As an adult, she feeds her addiction in every spare second. She spent years trying to build a "sensible" career, working in bookstores, recruitment, resource management, administration, and as a travel agent before finally conceding defeat and devoting herself to the world of romance novels.

Louisa has a long list of places first discovered in books that she wants to visit, and every so often she overcomes her loathing of jet lag and takes a trip that charges her imagination. She lives in Melbourne, Australia, where she whines about the weather for most of the year while secretly admitting she'll probably never move.

http://www.louisamasters.com

www.ingramcontent.com/pod-product-compliance
Lightning Source LLC
Chambersburg PA
CBHW030906060726
47591CB00005B/1432